J's Diary

The first girl's death was an accident.

I lifted my pen off of the paper and thought for a bit. My pen was poised to cross it out – the impulse trembled up my arm – but in the end, I left the sentence as it was.

I don't really know why I started writing this diary, account, whatever you'd call it. I suppose I wanted a record of what's happened in my life since the first one. Ever since I realised what I had to do to become complete – to unfold into a whole person rather than inhabit the empty shell of one – there's been another urge, almost as strong: the need to write down *why* I do the things I do. I'm not trying to justify anything to anyone, in the unlikely event that someone reads these diaries. The key thing, I suppose, is to be true to myself, to be truthful when I'm talking to myself as I am here, setting down these words. That's the only meaningful thing to do. If I'd only been true to myself from an early age, none of the bad things would have happened. Or maybe they would. Who knows?

So, in the interest of truth, the first death wasn't really an *accident*. I've just checked my dictionary and the definition of "accident" is something like *an unfortunate event that happens unintentionally*. Her death was certainly unfortunate – for her – and it was, at the time, unintentional. I didn't plan it; I didn't spends hours and days fantasising about bringing it about as I have done with the other ones. So you could say it was accidental, I suppose, although I'd have a hard time convincing a jury.

It won't come to that, though. Now I'm getting good at this. It's a new skill, as well as a calling, and I've always been a fast learner. It makes me shiver in anticipation when I think that I could go on like this, year after year, getting better each time. Each time more perfect and more fulfilling than the last one. All those girls out there, for me. None of them have any idea that I am watching and waiting, waiting for the next time...the next death. None of them have any idea because I am in disguise. They don't fear me. Quite the opposite. It makes it twice as fun. Fun. That's certainly a surprising choice of words, especially for me, but that's what it is. It *is* fun – as well as the greatest pleasure I've ever

Imago

A Kate Redman Mystery: Book 3

Celina Grace

known. Why don't they tell you this? Why do they lie? I feel like I'm the keeper of a secret only a few have discovered.

I know the next time will be soon; I've learnt to recognise the signs. I think I even know who it will be. She's oblivious, of course, just as she should be. All the time, I watch and wait, and she has no idea, none at all. And why would she? I'm disguised as myself, the very best disguise there is.

Chapter One

Kate ran.

Her breath rasped in and out of her lungs; her leg muscles burned. A drop of sweat rolled into the corner of her dry mouth. It felt as if she'd been running forever, weaving among the people on the pavements, the shock of her feet hitting the concrete reverberating through her muscles. Every fibre of her being cried out for her to stop, but she couldn't – she was afraid. The man was a sadist, a brutal sadist. She struggled on up a slight incline, her face burning, her lungs crying out for air. At the top of the hill, she had to stop, bent double, gasping for breath. The man following her at an effortless, loping run drew up alongside her.

"Come on, Kate. We've still got two miles to go."

"I can't," gasped Kate, when she had enough oxygen in her lungs to speak. "I'll be sick."

"You won't."

"Will."

The man appeared to relent. "All right. Take a two-minute breather."

Kate staggered over to a convenient bench and fell onto it. She put her roasting face down between her knees.

"Can't – do – this," she said, between gasps.

Detective Sergeant Mark Olbeck sat down beside her and stretched his legs out in front of him.

"It's only a bloody half marathon, for God's sake," he said. "Thirteen miles. It's nothing."

Kate sat back up again, marginally more comfortable, although still breathing hard.

"I'm too – unfit. Someone else will have to – do it."

"You'll *get* fit. That's the whole point of us going out running. Come on, you said you'd do it. It's for charity, remember."

"I can't get fit enough in three weeks."

"Well that's all the time you've got. You've got to be part of the team. If you pull out now, we won't have enough people."

Kate knew this was right. The Abbeyford Charity Half Marathon team from the police station had consisted of Olbeck, Detective Constable Theo Marsh and Detective Constable Ravinder Cheetam until Theo had broken his ankle playing football and had to drop out.

"There's Jerry. And Jane."

"You know as well as I do that Jane's got two

small children and no partner. She can't go out in the evenings at the drop of a hat. And Jerry would probably have a coronary or something if we made him run, the poor old bugger."

Kate leant back against the back of the bench and closed her eyes. She knew all this already, which made her feel even worse about her lack of enthusiasm.

"Don't get comfortable," warned Olbeck. "Come on. On we go."

Kate heaved the deepest sigh her abused lungs could muster. Then she lurched to her feet, and they jogged on through the streets of Abbeyford.

They stopped at the bridge that spanned the river Avon, leaning against the stone parapet and watching the glittering waters slide beneath them. It was a beautiful summer's day, the sky blue but wisped with a filmy curtain of white cloud, the sun gaining in strength by the hour.

"You know, Mark, I'm really not sure I can do this," puffed Kate. She leant her head on her folded arms for a moment and then raised it, looking out at the sparkling water.

"You'll be fine," said Olbeck. "And you'll feel very proud of yourself when you finish."

"I've done plenty of things I'm already proud of," said Kate. "I don't feel that putting one foot in front of the other very quickly qualifies as any kind of great achievement."

Mark grinned. "God, you're narky today."

"It's the unaccustomed blood rushing to my head."

There was a muffled buzzing from Mark's back pocket. He fished his phone out, frowned and answered the call.

"Hello sir. No, we're not doing anything."

Kate waited, knowing it was something serious. She had that familiar feeling she got every time a new case began: tension, anxiety and yes, shamefully, a little bit of excitement, which was tempered with relief – at least she wouldn't have to do any more running that day.

Olbeck said goodbye and put the phone back in his pocket. His partner raised her eyebrows.

"That was Anderton."

"So I gathered. What is it?"

"Dead woman, down by the canal. We've been called in."

"Let's go, then."

Abbeyford was a large market town in the southwest of England. In addition to the river Avon, one of several so named in the country, the town also had a canal running through it. In earlier times, goods had been brought to the town from neighbouring cities, and canal boats pulled by horses moved slowly along the paths by the water to be unloaded at the tiny docks. The canal freight trade had long since gone, and the canal docks in Abbeyford had gradually fallen into disrepair and, eventually, disrepute. The warehouse windows were all broken, the glass in the few remaining panes dulled with dirt and moss. A long-ago fire had gutted one of the buildings, leaving its blackened girders exposed like the charred bones of an animal. Rubbish, dead leaves and dirt were heaped in every corner.

Kate had never been to the area before; she was barely aware of its existence. Perhaps the other Abbeyford residents had a similar knowledge of this part of town, and this was why the killer had chosen to dump the body here. Or had killer and victim met here?

As it turned out, Kate wasn't off the jogging hook after all. She and Olbeck were close enough to the site to make their way there on foot, and Olbeck had insisted that they run, "to get in some more training." Kate arrived at the scene knowing that her face was tomato-red and that her tracksuit was stained with patches of sweat, but after one look at the huddled body of the woman on the ground, these minor concerns faded away.

Scene of Crime officers had already erected the tent that hid the body from prying eyes. Kate and Olbeck ducked under the flap that covered the entrance. The victim was a small, thin woman, with long, dark hair tied tightly back in a high ponytail. She lay on her side, curled in a foetal position, her back to the detectives. One dirty-soled foot was bare; the scuffed silver ballet pump that had fallen from it rested a few inches away. Kate couldn't see any obvious wounds, although the mottled, bare legs were spattered with small amounts of blood.

She studied the scene as intently as she could in the short time that she had, taking in everything that she could see. *Get a feel for the scene*, Anderton was always telling them. *It's amazing what you can pick up without even realising. It can come in very handy as the case progresses.* Kate knew she would never again have this first impression, so she observed with laser-intensity focus, trying to burn the image onto her retinas and into her mind.

Detective Chief Inspector Anderton was there along with Detective Constables Jerry Hindley and Ravinder Cheetam – Rav to his friends and colleagues. The three of them were in a huddle, talking quietly, whilst behind them, the scene was being preserved, photographed and otherwise documented by the Scene of Crime officers. Anderton looked up as Kate and Olbeck approached.

"You got here commendably quickly," was his opening remark. "Glad to see all this running's starting to pay off."

Olbeck gave Kate a 'you *see*?' look but said nothing. He nodded at Jerry and Rav.

"Let's go outside," said Anderton. "Too many people in here."

Outside, the air felt fresh and the sunlight was warm and welcoming on Kate's upturned face.

"What's been happening?" she asked.

"The body was discovered this morning," said Anderton. "A couple of hours ago, so that makes it, what – twelve thirty or so?"

"Who found it?" asked Kate.

"Two young lads. They were a bit reticent about why they were down here in the first place. Probably here to do some tagging or something. They're back at the station at the moment, giving their statements."

"Cause of death?" asked Olbeck.

"We don't yet know. Stanton should be able to tell us more when he's finished – talk of the devil—" Anderton looked up as the white-clad figure of the pathologist emerged from the tent. "Stanton. Stanton!" he called. "What's the quick and dirty?"

Doctor Andrew Stanton joined the group, brightening a little as he realised Kate was amongst them. He had an undisguised admiration for her, which always led to a day's worth of teasing from Olbeck after the three of them met.

"Hi guys. Hi Kate," he added, with special, caressing attention. The other men grinned, and

Kate managed to grit her teeth and smile politely at the same time.

"What have we got?" asked Anderton.

Stanton immediately became professional.

"Stab wounds, several of them, mostly through the lower thoracic region. Stomach and lower chest."

Anderton shook his head.

"Definitely one for us, then. Oh well. Any sign of sexual assault?"

"Difficult to tell. I'll be able to give you a better answer once we've done the PM."

"Right," said Anderton. "Stab wounds. That puts another possible spin on things." He didn't elaborate on what this spin could be. "Any chance of fixing the time of death?"

Stanton shrugged.

"Probably sometime early in the morning, very early. Two or three o'clock. You know I can't be accurate at this stage. You'll have to wait for the PM."

"It gives us a starting point," said Anderton, briefly. "Okay, thanks, Andrew. We'll speak later."

Once Doctor Stanton had left, Anderton ducked into the tent, quickly followed by Rav and Olbeck. Kate found herself standing alone with Jerry Hindley, and her heart sank a little. Jerry was the colleague she knew and liked the least. From the very start of her career at Abbeyford, he'd made it plain that he didn't like her. She'd asked Olbeck and Theo why this might be, and they'd explained that it was probably jealously. "You got the promotion he'd been angling for, Kate," Olbeck had said, and although this sounded plausible, it seemed strange that he'd still be acting hurt and resentful two years later. Again she reminded herself that she didn't care about the opinion of someone so petty and sexist. Occasionally she'd attempt to be friendly, wondering whether he'd ever respond in the same way. She tried again now.

"What do you think happened, Jerry?"

He sighed in an irritated manner. "Didn't you hear the guv? We don't know anything other than what you just heard."

Kate said nothing more. Why did she bother? Was she trying to make him like her? Why? She didn't care about his opinion, did she?

She was relieved to see the other officers exit the tent and make their way back to where she stood.

"Do we have an ID on the victim yet, sir?" Kate asked Anderton, provoking an irritated sigh from Jerry. She ignored him.

Anderton shook his head.

"There's no ID at all on the body. No cards, no purse, no bag."

"Really? That's strange. You'd expect her to have a purse at least, even if she didn't use a handbag."

"Exactly," said Anderton. "It was almost certainly

removed from the body by our perpetrator." He looked at the still surface of the canal. "We're going to have to have that searched. It could easily be in there, as well as the murder weapon."

Olbeck was glancing around at the buildings surrounding them.

"Any cameras here?" he asked. "CCTV footage would help."

"I can't see any," said Kate, scanning the scene. "It doesn't look the sort of place where people would care about vandalism or theft."

"Right, well," said Anderton. "We need to start digging. We don't know whether the murder actually took place here, although from the blood found at the scene, it seems likely. We don't know who the victim is. We don't know what the murder weapon was – yes, some kind of knife, but what kind? We're currently operating from a standpoint of complete ignorance, and that's not a position I like to be in." He paused for breath. "Let's get back to HQ, and we'll take it from there."

Chapter Two

"THE WEAPON THAT CREATED THESE wounds was unusual," said Doctor Telling. She was washing her hands as she spoke, speaking over her shoulder to Kate, who had arrived too late for the actual post mortem. "Very unusual in this kind of case."

"Really? It was a knife, I assume?"

"Oh, yes, that's without doubt. But a knife with a serrated edge. A steak knife or something like that."

"A *steak* knife?" Kate's eyebrows rose. "That is odd."

Doctor Telling finished drying her long, thin fingers. She smiled her unearthly smile. "Yes, I don't believe I've ever come across one used as a murder weapon before. Have you found it, by the way?"

Kate shook her head. "No. No sign of it."

"It should be easy to match it to the wounds if you do."

"Right. Anything else that's pertinent? I know I'll get your report but—"

"Quite a lot." Doctor Telling was taking off her

stained white coat. She dropped it into what was obviously a laundry basket. Underneath she wore a rather incongruous floral blouse. "She was a drug user – injection marks all over her. She'd had at least one child. And while I didn't find any semen, there were traces of condom lubricant."

"Hmm," said Kate. "So our perpetrator is savvy enough to cover up. Was she raped?"

Doctor Telling shrugged her thin shoulders. "Possibly. It's unusual for a rapist to use a condom, but it's not unheard of. There's no obvious damage, no bruising or abrasions. It's hard to tell. Do you have an ID on the victim yet?"

"We're running the fingerprints through the database now."

"I think it's likely that the victim was a prostitute."

"Based on what you've told me, I think you're right."

The Abbeyford police station was undergoing something of a renovation. The reception area was now equipped with some fairly convincing wood-grain laminate (Kate deplored the use of laminate but could see that polished wooden floorboards were out of the question, simply as a matter of cost) and had been repainted a fresh and sprightly green. The interview rooms had also been repainted, and Anderton's office now had new carpet.

The room currently being renovated was the

team's main office, which meant that everyone had been required to grumblingly pack up all their files and office paraphernalia and shift all their computers to a different room. At least it gave everyone the opportunity to complain about the unfamiliar office chairs and the distance to the coffee machine. It also meant that team meetings now tended to take place in Anderton's freshly carpeted office, which hadn't really been designed for large meetings. There was always a scrimmage for chairs. Today, Kate had successfully acquired one over by the window. She tried to flex her stiff legs, which were still aching from yesterday's exercise session.

Now that meetings were held in his office, Anderton was unable to start things off, as he used to do, by crashing through the door like a human whirlwind. He was also clearly unable to pace about as much as he wanted to. It made Kate chuckle inwardly to see him start out with a firm stride only to bring himself up short as he realised the limitations of the space available.

"Right, team, let's get on. Excuse the by-now-familiar cramped conditions. Anyone know when we move back to the incident room?" No one knew, although Jane tentatively volunteered that it might be next week. "God, let's hope so. Can't work under these conditions. Anyway, where were we?"

Anderton came to a stop in front of the much-reduced set of whiteboards that had migrated over to his office during the renovation. Several crime scene photographs were pinned up already, demonstrating the curled shape of the dead woman, one shoe lying beside her pale, dirty foot.

"You'll be pleased to know that we're now much further forward than we were this morning – we have ID'd the victim. Amanda Renkin, more commonly known as Mandy Renkin. Twenty-six years old, a known prostitute and drug user. The usual, sad story: chaotic childhood, in and out of care homes. Pregnant at seventeen, baby removed from her care shortly after birth." Kate flinched, still unable to hear those words without some sort of emotional reaction. Would she ever be able to?

Anderton continued.

"Convictions for soliciting and drug use. Nothing that comes as any great surprise, poor woman."

"Did she work alone?" asked Olbeck. "I mean, did she have a pimp or something?"

"That's something we'll have to find out. We don't even know if she worked the streets. She may have had a place that she used. Something we need to find out. Talk to some of the usual girls, see if they can tell us anything. Jane, Theo, get onto the CCTV, if there is any in the area. If not, look at what's nearest, see if you can find anything. Jerry, Rav, if there are any residential areas near the crime scene, talk to people. See if they saw or heard anything."

Kate raised her hand.

"Shall Mark and I do her address, sir?"

Anderton nodded. "Yep, first thing. See what you can find. Talk to her relatives, talk to her friends, if she had any. Now I'm sure I don't need to remind you all that the most likely perpetrator in this kind of crime is an ex-partner or even a current partner. Don't let the fact that she was a prostitute blind you to that. Dig into her background. Did she have a husband or boyfriend? Who was the father of her child?"

Anderton came to the edge of his desk and hoisted himself up, sitting on the edge with his legs swinging. Somehow, the boyish movement went straight to Kate's heart. Suddenly moved, she blinked and looked away.

That moment, though it had been brief, kept recurring to Kate when she was back at her desk. She had begun the slow, wearisome task of checking her share of the background facts that Anderton had brought up. She'd long been aware of her attraction to her boss and had managed to keep it a secret from him, from the rest of the team and, with surprising success, from herself as well.

She gave herself the usual stern talking to, reciting an inner monologue that pointed out the sad predictability of being attracted to your boss; the foolishness that resulted from such a breach of professional behaviour; and the fact that it could only lead to humiliation, scorn and misery. How pursuing her feelings would be professional and probably social suicide. Staring blankly at her computer screen while the same old words went round and round in her head, Kate could only think one thing: *I don't care. I still want him.*

With a massive effort, she shoved those treacherous feelings back down into the depths of her subconscious and turned her attention back to the case.

"Get anything?" asked Olbeck from across the desks.

Kate tapped the keys to print out some data.

"Got an address. Looks like some sort of hostel or something like that. Saint Andrews Mission, Church Road, Arbuthon Green."

"That's a homeless charity, I think." said Olbeck, getting up. He perched himself on the edge of Kate's desk and she realised he was dressed in a tracksuit. "Catholic. Shall we go and check it out?"

"Yes," said Kate, standing up. She swung her car keys in an ostentatious circle. "And we're *driving*."

"Fine," said Olbeck, grinning. "Just means we'll have to do an extra training session tomorrow. No drama."

Kate said nothing but suppressed a silent scream.

St Andrews Mission was located in what had

obviously once been a village school, Victorian-built, with the usual attention to decorative detail and handsome arched windows. What had once been the playground at the front of the building was now paved over to make space for several cars to park. Kate was pleased to see the old school bell still remained up under the eaves and pointed it out to Olbeck as they got out of the car.

The reception area was painted in industrial green. A low, scuffed table sat by the front desk with a variety of leaflets, advertising counselling services, mother and baby groups, drug and alcohol support groups. A small number of battered chairs stood against the wall, and the reception desk was located behind a glass partition. Behind the reception desk, there was a door with a security key code pad on it.

The grey-haired woman, dressed in a white blouse, who staffed the reception desk looked up as the officers approached.

Kate introduced herself and Olbeck. The woman looked apprehensive.

"Oh yes, we did speak on the phone earlier, I remember," she said. "I'm Margaret Paling."

"Do you run this place?" asked Kate.

"Oh no, dear, I'm just one of the volunteers. You'll need to talk to Father Michael, but he's out at the moment."

"We'd like to have a quick chat with you, Mrs

Paling, if we may. I understand you knew Mandy Renkin?"

Margaret Paling nodded. She was fingering a rather lovely rhinestone brooch pinned to the lapel of her blouse.

"It's Miss Paling," she said. "I'm not married. But I'd be happy to have a chat. Would you like to come through, and I'll make us some tea?"

Kate and Olbeck were ushered through the security door into a lounge-type area, which sported several worn sofas and armchairs. There was a bookcase with a small selection of second-hand books, a magazine rack stuffed with lots of dog-eared celebrity gossip magazines and a box full of children's toys.

"We'll go through to Father Michael's office," said Margaret. "The residents aren't normally up this early, but if you want to talk privately it's best we use the office." She saw Kate's expression. "Oh, I know. Ten thirty in the morning is isn't very early, but these girls – well, they're not very *disciplined*, shall we say. Mind you, having said that, a couple of them are actually in work at the moment, and they're out, obviously, and the children are in school."

"Children?" said Olbeck.

Margaret nodded as she opened the door to a small office.

"We have two family rooms here," she said. "Of

course, they're always in use. In fact, we're full to the brim at the moment."

She bustled around, making the tea. Kate had expected to see the usual chipped and battered mugs, milk in a plastic bottle and sugar clumped together in a metal bowl. Instead, Margaret set out a rather nice old tea set, complete with milk jug and dainty sugar bowl. A wisp of steam rose from the spout of the teapot.

"What lovely china," said Kate. "Royal Doulton, isn't it?"

Margaret looked gratified.

"That's right," she said. "Been in my family for years. May as well get some use out of it." She looked as though she was about to say more for a moment, but she didn't. She handed Kate and Olbeck their cups. It had been a long time since Kate had drunk tea from a delicate china cup and saucer. It was good tea, hot and strong.

"You knew Mandy Renkin?" asked Olbeck.

Margaret nodded, fingering her brooch again.

"I knew her, but not very well. She hadn't been here long and it seemed as though—" She faltered, looking awkward. "Well, it's not for me to say, but it did seem as though she might not have been here very much longer. We're very strict on our no alcohol and no drug use policy here – we have to be – and, well..."

"Mandy was using drugs?" asked Kate.

Margaret nodded again. "I don't know for sure, but I know that Father Michael had, well, *words* with her to that very end. They had quite an argument, actually."

"When was this?"

"I'm not sure. I only heard it about it from someone else, one of the other volunteers. Perhaps two weeks ago? I couldn't say for sure."

"We'll speak to Father Michael when he comes back," said Kate. "He runs the hostel, then?"

"Yes, he's the supervisor here. It's a Church-funded charity."

Olbeck carefully placed his empty cup back on its saucer and transferred both to what was obviously Father Michael's desk.

"Could we have a look at Mandy's room, Miss Paling?"

Margaret looked worried but nodded.

"Yes, of course. I'll take you there right away."

"When do you expect Father Michael back?" asked Kate, as Margaret led them back through the sitting room, through another door, along several corridors, across a paved courtyard and finally into another building, a modern block of apartments.

"I couldn't say for sure. Perhaps after lunch?" Margaret stopped before a door numbered 14. She unlocked it and pushed it open gently.

"This is Mandy's room."

Chapter Three

THE TWO OFFICERS STEPPED INSIDE the dim room. The blind at the window was pulled down and the air inside smelt stale. Kate nodded at Margaret in a way she hoped was polite but dismissive.

"Thank you, Miss Paling. We'll take it from here and come and find you when we're done."

"Yes – yes, of course."

Margaret pulled the door shut behind her as she left. Kate waited until her footsteps had faded from hearing. Then she tossed a pair of gloves to Olbeck.

"Let's get some light in here, at least."

Olbeck let the blind roll up with a snap that sounded very loud in the silent room. Kate looked around. The room had an institutional look: grey carpet, patchy woodchip on the walls, a duvet cover in navy blue with a matching pillowcase on the one, thin pillow. Still, she imagined beggars couldn't be choosers: if it were a choice between this dull but functional room and the streets, Kate knew which she would chose.

Mandy Renkin had only had a few possessions, which was not unusual for someone who was shuttling between B&Bs, homeless hostels and other temporary accommodation. There were some clothes in the little chest of drawers by the window; it didn't take long for Kate to sort through them. Cheap and badly made, for the most part, although there was one obviously hand-knitted jumper that drew Kate's attention. She picked it up, noting the cable stitch, the good quality wool. Had Mandy's mother or grandmother made this for her? Or had she picked it up in a charity shop somewhere? Kate said as much to Olbeck.

"We need to find out about her family," said Olbeck. "Rav's digging into her records back at the station."

Kate nodded. She moved to the small bookcase that stood by the single bed. There were only five books contained therein. Four were romance novels in shabby pink and purple covers. One was an old copy of – Kate blinked and picked it up – Charles Dickens' *Great Expectations*. A strange juxtaposition with the other reading matter. Kate turned to the flyleaf of the book and saw the bookplate. *Awarded to Amanda Renkin for Excellence in English*. The date on the bookplate was twelve years ago. Kate stared unseeing for a moment, picturing the fourteen-year-old Mandy, smart in school uniform, accepting the pristine book from a school Governor, or perhaps the Headteacher. *Great Expectations*. Thinking of Mandy's eventual fate, the title was the cruellest possible cosmic joke. How had a smart schoolgirl gone from receiving a school prize at fourteen to dead on the streets at twenty six?

Kate replaced the book on the shelf, carefully. She had these moments in every case, where professional immunity failed. In every case, there were a few moments of pain, brief but excruciating, like a long silver pin being plunged into her heart. She'd told Olbeck that once and he'd said, unexpectedly, *I know, it hurts, but it's good that you feel that, Kate. You know you're in trouble if you ever stop feeling like that.*

Kate sighed, loud enough for Olbeck to look up from his own search. He opened his mouth to ask her what was wrong but shut it again as she shook her head, mutely.

There was a hesitant knock on the door, and Margaret Paling opened it and poked her head tentatively into the room.

"Father Michael is back," she said. "I've let him know you want to talk to him."

"Thanks," said Kate. "If you could ask him to come here, perhaps?"

"Yes, of course. One moment."

They heard the tap of her heels as she walked away back down the corridor. Kate turned her attention back to the small chest of drawers by the bed. There was nothing in the bottom drawer, a jumble of socks and underwear in the middle drawer, and in the top one, several packets of painkillers, crumpled tissues, a half-full cigarette packet and a framed photograph. Kate picked up up carefully. A woman – girl, really – who was clearly Mandy Renkin smiled out at her from the frame. Her cheek was pressed to the face of a baby boy, perhaps three months old or so, toothless mouth open in a drooling, gummy grin. Another of those pins pierced Kate's heart, and she blinked several times, swallowing hard.

There was another knock at the door.

"I heard you wanted to see me," said the tall, thin man who entered the room, obviously Father Michael. Olbeck and Kate heaved themselves to a standing position, pulled off their gloves and shook hands, introducing themselves.

Father Michael looked about the room and sighed.

"It's not much," he said apologetically. "We're always short of funds. It's getting worse now, with the benefit cuts of course. But we do what we can for these girls."

"I'm sure you do, sir," said Kate, sizing him up. He was probably younger than she'd first thought, late fifties perhaps, with a soft brown beard tinged with grey and narrow, sloping shoulders. His voice was unexpectedly deep and melodious – she could imagine he preached very well.

"We're trying to find out as much as we can about Mandy Renkin," said Olbeck. "Obviously, the more we know about her, the easier it is to find out who might have killed her. What can you tell us about her?"

Father Michael sat down on the edge of the bed and clasped his hands together.

"I hadn't known her for long," he said. "She'd not been here for more than a handful of weeks, only a month or so. Her social worker had passed the details of the Mission to Mandy at one of their meetings. Mandy had recently been released from prison, and I think she thought it might be a bit of a fresh start for her."

"What was she in prison for?"

"I'm not sure exactly. Soliciting or shoplifting or something fairly minor. It was only a short sentence, a matter of weeks."

"And when she was released she came straight here?"

Father Michael shook his head. "She was briefly in a hostel – a few days or so. I understood that Mandy had managed to complete a drug rehabilitation course in prison. That was why we were able to accept her here. We're very strict on there being no drugs and alcohol allowed on site and anyone found using or supplying them will be asked to leave."

Kate nodded. "Yes, Miss Paling said. She also mentioned that you and Mandy had had some sort of altercation recently. Can you tell us about that?"

Father Michael's rather thick eyebrows rose.

"An altercation?"

"Yes. An argument, a quarrel," said Kate, deliberately misunderstanding his repetition of the word. "Is that true?"

There was a moment's silence.

"Well, I suppose you could call it that," said Father Michael reluctantly. "I'm surprised at Margaret... There wasn't really much to tell."

Kate and Olbeck said nothing. They were skilled in letting the silence spool out for long enough that the person they were interviewing needed then to fill it.

"I found out that Mandy was using drugs again. Or, let me be accurate, I was informed she was using drugs again, and I wanted to hear what she had to say for herself."

"And what did she say?"

There was a moment's hesitation, so brief that Kate almost missed it.

"She told me it was a lie. That she wasn't using drugs again, and she didn't know who had told me that."

"Who had told you that?"

"One of the other women here. Claudia Smith."

Kate saw Olbeck scribble that name down in his notepad.

"Did you believe Mandy?"

Father Michael's narrow shoulders hunched for a moment. Then he shook his head slowly.

"I'm afraid I didn't believe her."

"You believed she was using drugs again?"

He nodded. "You get to know the signs. And I must say, I know very well when someone is lying to me."

"When did you have this argument?" asked Olbeck.

"Not long ago. Perhaps four or five days ago? I told her she couldn't stay here if she was using drugs, reminded her of the rules, you know."

"And how did Mandy react?"

Father Michael sighed.

"I'm afraid she became very foul-mouthed and abusive and ended up slamming the door to her room and locking herself in."

"I see," said Kate. "And what happened after that?"

"How do you mean?"

"I mean, how did you react?"

Father Michael half smiled.

"If you mean, was I upset by our argument, then of course I was, a little. But the most important thing about running a charity of this kind is that you have to, at some level, remain detached. Otherwise you just get carried away with the – well, the awfulness of some people's lives. So, I suppose I mentally shrugged my shoulders and went back to my office."

"What would have happened to Mandy if she'd left the Mission?" asked Olbeck.

"We would have tried to find her a place at a B&B or something. Perhaps another hostel. By evicting her from the Mission, we would have been making her effectively homeless, so the council would have had an obligation to house her."

"But that didn't happen?"

Father Michael stared at him.

"No, it didn't," he said. "Because she died before it came to that."

"Where you upset by her death, Father?"

The thick eyebrows jerked upwards.

"What a question, officer. The death of a young girl – of course I was upset. Of course I was. We were all devastated."

Kate stood up, thinking that they had enough to go on by now.

"Just one more thing, sir. Could you tell us your whereabouts on the night of the fourteenth of June?"

"That's when Mandy died?"

"Could you answer the question please, sir?"

Father Michael considered for a moment.

"Well – I'm afraid I was at home. I usually am in the evening."

"Can anyone confirm that, sir?"

Father Michael shook his head slowly.

"I'm afraid not," he said. He looked worried. "I live alone, you see. I didn't talk to anyone—"

"What's your address, Father?" asked Olbeck. He wrote down the answer as the priest answered him.

"Twenty six Lavender Street, Charlock."

"That's fine, sir," said Kate. "We'll leave our cards, and I'm sure we'll be back to ask you some more questions. If you think of anything at all that you think might be relevant, please don't hesitate to get in touch."

Father Michael nodded, his face serious. He stood back a little to allow them access to the door.

"Do you have any idea who might have done this dreadful thing?" he asked, just as they were leaving.

"Our enquiries are continuing, sir," said Kate, the usual response.

"I hope you catch him."

Kate and Olbeck said nothing, but smiled neutrally before saying goodbye.

J's Diary

I ORDERED THE FIRST GIRL ONLINE.

It's amazing if you think of it – how you can put in a request for a human being as easily as you might order a new television or even your week's shopping. Click a mouse and put something in your virtual basket: milk, sausages, chicken breasts, a woman. Just another type of commodity. Just another type of meat.

I purposely used a site I'd never used before or since, directing the responses to a new Hotmail address I'd set up specially. The credit card payment was more difficult. In the end, I used one of Mother's, thinking perhaps I could say it had been stolen if it were ever traced back to me. Of course, at that time, I wasn't foreseeing any of the kind of trouble that happened that night. I merely wanted to avoid any potential embarrassment. God forbid that anyone would recognise me. So, a strange agency and a strange girl was what I wanted.

I was very nervous before she arrived. It had

only been a few weeks since Mother had died, and I still felt as if she were going to suddenly appear at any moment. Several times, I thought I heard her faltering footsteps in the bedrooms above me, and once, after a creak in the hallway, I was convinced that her head with its puff of white hair and her piercing steel-grey eyes would appear around the living room doorway momentarily. I even froze for an instant, clutching the arms of the chair, before realising how stupid I was being. There was no one there, of course. I kept telling myself, *She's dead. She's gone. She's dead. She's gone.*

So, the night the girl arrived, I was extremely jumpy. I prowled the rooms downstairs, glancing nervously at the clock as the hands inched around to 9:00 p.m. I'd got everything ready, and for the first time ever in my life, I actually felt like myself. I actually felt as if it *could* work. I regarded myself in the hallway mirror, pulling my tie straight. Yes. *It will work*, I told myself. *You can do it*.

The doorbell rang at that moment, shattering the silence in the house, and I'd actually jumped. Then I hurried to the door and opened it as quickly as possible. I'd taken the lightbulb out of the porch light socket, but I was still suddenly terrified that the neighbours would be looking out of their front window and wondering what a tart was doing ringing my doorbell.

I don't know why but I'd imagined a girl in heels,

a leopard-skin coat, red lipstick. Stupid, really. The woman standing on the doorstep was short, thin, and dressed in a shabby blue fleece and skinny jeans and trainers. She looked a most unlikely prostitute, but as I hurried her into the house, I could see the fleece was unzipped slightly and a curve of damp cleavage visible beneath the zip. I felt a welcome surge of excitement.

I closed the door behind her.

"What's your name?" she asked, peering through the gloom at me.

"John."

Even in the dim light, I could see her lip curl. I think she knew it wasn't my real name.

"John, eh? Right you are, *John*. What d'you want to do?"

Funny, all this time I'd been frantically waiting for this moment, the moment of actually doing what it was I'd wanted to do for so long. And now that it was here and on the verge of happening, I found myself backpedalling.

"Do you want a drink or something?" I asked. My voice sounded tremulous – I despised myself. Why couldn't I sound forthright and authoritative? In my head, I could see Mother's sneer, the same sneer that had confronted me almost every day of my life.

I could feel my hands clench.

"Yeah, all right," said the tart, and I gestured towards the kitchen.

I'll come clean now and say I was already quite drunk. I was nervous – so nervous – and I had to have something to calm my nerves. I'd heard of alcohol having the wrong kind of effect, of course I had, but I was in such a state before she arrived that I thought I'd risk it. I'd already had about three large whiskies before the door went.

The tart strutted into the kitchen like she owned the place. I'd kept the strip light off and the only light came from a candle I'd placed on the kitchen windowsill. The girl stopped when she saw it and I could see she was momentarily disconcerted. Perhaps she was thinking that I only wanted to do the romance thing. I'd heard of men doing that – hiring tarts to pretend to be their girlfriends for the night.

I didn't want the romance thing. I wanted everything.

I poured her a whisky without asking her what she wanted. She sipped and made a face, as if it wasn't the best aged Laphroaig. After Mother died, almost the very day she died, I'd gone to the sacred drinks cabinet, where unopened bottles had stood ever since Father had left, and broken the seal on the first one I could find. There were only a few left now.

After her first sip, she knocked it back in one swallow, grimacing as if it were medicine.

"All right," she said. "I ain't got all night. Let's get going."

"R-right—" I began, but before I could say any more, the tart said something like "Fucking dark in here" and snapped on the light switch.

There was a moment of blinding dazzle after the strip light stuttered on. Both of us recoiled slightly, blinking. I had time for a second of outrage about the fact that she'd just taken it upon herself, in someone else's house, to dictate the light levels. It was *my* house. Who did she think she was?

I only had time for a second of thought because at that moment she saw me clearly. A moment later, a harsh disbelieving laugh rang out into the kitchen.

She was laughing at me.

For some reason I thought of Mother and her sneer that was half a smile. Before I could even open my mouth to tell her to shut up, I flinched backwards against the kitchen counter and suddenly the steak knife was in my hand.

"Shut up!" I hissed, and I thrust the knife forward.

Did I just mean to scare her? I don't know. All I wanted was for that mocking laughter to stop. The knife sank into her stomach, piercing the fleece. The tart said, "Oh," a sound of surprise rather than pain. We both looked down at the knife protruding from her belly, just to the right of the zip. I still had hold of the handle.

There was a moment of silence. Then she drew in her breath and screamed, shatteringly loud.

Panicked, I snatched my hand back and drove the knife forward again, not caring where I hit her. I just had to stop the noise. But the strangest thing happened. As the blade sank into her, again and again, I – well, I...

La petit mort, they call it. I was swept away, lost, carried away on a release so powerful that when it finally stopped, I believed for a second I had died too.

When I came back to reality, I was face down on the body of the tart, my hand still clenched around the handle of the steak knife that was buried deeply inside her. I was wet with blood and not just with blood. I rolled over onto my back, next to the body on the kitchen floor, gasping for breath and holding the knife against my chest like a talisman.

Chapter Four

"DON'T FORGET WE'RE TRAINING AGAIN tonight," said Olbeck as they got into the car.

Kate gritted her teeth.

"I hadn't," she said, after a moment. "That's all we do, every night. Every day and every night."

"You'll thank me," said Olbeck breezily. "Tell you what. How about we do our run and then you come over for dinner with me and Jeff?"

Kate was waiting to join the main road. She used the time spent gauging the oncoming traffic to think over Olbeck's suggestion. It was tempting. Jeff was Olbeck's partner – Kate kept thinking of him as Olbeck's 'new' partner, despite the fact they'd been together for just over a year. Jeff was thirty-eight, an academic specialising in sports sciences and a fitness fanatic. Kate knew who to blame for Olbeck's newfound fitness regime and his punishing insistence that Kate join in. Still, it was a minor niggle.

Jeff was warm, witty, nice-looking and a

supportive and easy-going boyfriend to her friend. She'd spent many an enjoyable evening with the two of them: at dinner parties, at the theatre, at a barbeque with mutual colleagues and at lazy Sunday brunches at the local pubs. Kate and Jeff got on very well and she could see that he and Olbeck were a loving and committed couple. And yet... And yet...she felt guilty thinking it, but she couldn't deny it. Occasionally she wished it was just her and Olbeck again, as it had been when he was single. She felt terrible for even thinking that, but at the same time, she couldn't help it. *You're jealous*, she told herself again. Not jealous because she wanted Olbeck for a *boyfriend*, for God's sake. But jealous because before Jeff appeared, it was just the two of them and now there were three and now Kate was the odd one out.

It was funny; for years she'd been happy with her own company. She hadn't wanted a partner. Unlike those women who said they were happy being single because they thought if they said that sort of thing out loud, the universe would reward them with the perfect man, Kate really had been happy being single. She had enough friends and enough interests to fill those odd hours that weren't taken up with work. But now...she sighed inwardly. Now, she felt differently. *I'm lonely. I want someone of my own. Not just someone. One person – Anderton.*

Kate drove ruminatively, tapping her fingers on the steering wheel.

"Let's go and talk to Claudia Smith now," she suggested. "She sounds like she knew Mandy, even if just in a casual way."

Olbeck nodded.

"Sounds like a plan."

There were two branches of Boots the Chemist in Abbeyford: a small shop on the outskirts of the town and a much larger central store in the main shopping area. Kate and Olbeck made their way to the latter, reasoning that Claudia Smith would be more likely to be found here. They were correct. After enquiring at one of the make-up booths, they were directed to a small bank of tills at the rear of the store.

Claudia Smith was easily picked out by her nametag. She was a small, dark-haired woman. As Kate observed her as they waited in the queue, she could see that Claudia was an excellent example of a basically pretty girl whose thick make-up, hugely volumised hair and overload of cheap jewellery negated rather than enhanced her attractiveness. Kate looked at the thick foundation, the hard line of black eyeliner, the orange fake tan and the huge, cheap silver hoops which dragged down Claudia's earlobes. Why did women *do* this to themselves? Did they genuinely think they looked better? Kate supposed they must. She had a secondary thought that those kind of women probably looked at her and wondered why she wasn't making more of herself.

Claudia's till became free and Kate and Olbeck stepped forward.

Kate introduced herself and her partner and flashed her card. Claudia's heavily outlined eyes widened.

"Don't be alarmed, Miss Smith," said Kate, realising that Claudia was also casting anxious glances towards an older woman hovering nearby who was clearly her line manager. "We'd just like to talk to you about Mandy Renkin. Would you like us to wait until you finish your shift?"

Claudia looked as though she wanted to agree but perhaps realised that asking the police to wait – loitering in the aisles, with her work colleagues giving them curious glances – would be worse. She shook her head and said "I'll just ask if I can go" before scurrying off to her line manager. Kate and Olbeck shifted a little to allow some shoppers to pass them by. After a minute or two, Claudia Smith came back, minus her Boots tabard and with a much studded and fringed but obviously cheap leather handbag.

Kate's conscience gave her a little nudge.

"I hope we haven't got you into trouble with your boss, Miss Smith," she said. "We'll be happy to talk to her if necessary, explain how things are."

Claudia shook her head. She was walking quite quickly, with her head down.

"It's all right," she said in a small voice. "Is it okay if we talk as we go along? It's just I have to pick my daughter up from the childminder's."

She barely looked out of her teens herself. How old was her daughter? Kate asked her.

"Four." Claudia's make-up-caked face brightened a little. "Her name's Madison."

"Perhaps we can give you a lift," suggested Olbeck. "That might give us a little time to talk."

When they were parked a few metres away from the childminder's house in Arbuthon Green, Olbeck turned off the engine and turned in his seat to face Claudia and Kate, who was sitting next to her on the back seat.

"We're trying to find out something more about Mandy," he said. "Were you friends with her?"

Claudia nodded nervously.

"We were at school together."

"And you've been friends ever since? You kept in touch after you left school?"

"Sort of. We both – we kind of both got into bad situations." Claudia's eyes flickered downwards. "Mandy started seeing this guy, Mike Fenton. He was really cool, everyone wanted to be with him, and Mandy was the one who ended up with him. But he was really bad news, got her into drugs and all that. She kind of dropped off the scene for a bit, for a long while actually."

Kate had been listening closely. She suppressed a sigh at the usual sad story: schoolgirl promise squandered on a boy who was a bad lot, someone who dragged you down into the gutter. And once you were there, it was almost impossible to climb out.

"Did Mandy get back in contact with you? How did you both end up at the Mission?"

Claudia fiddled with her earrings.

"We kind of kept in touch, off and on," she said. Her gaze dropped again. "She was a good mate to me. She helped me out when – when I needed it. She'd got off the drugs then, left Mike and was kind of getting herself back together again."

"When was this, Claudia?"

"I dunno. About two years ago."

"Was Mandy working as a prostitute then?"

Claudia's orange-hued face went faintly pink.

"I dunno," she said, again. "We didn't really talk about stuff like that."

"But she was kind to you?"

Claudia nodded. "She was there for me when I need her. Gave me some money, helped me—" She stopped for a moment. "She helped me get out."

Olbeck shifted a little in his seat. "What happened, Claudia?"

The girl kept her eyes down and spoke haltingly.

A sad tale of a relationship that seemed to start off well, an accidental pregnancy, an older man who, when his partner was at her most vulnerable, decided to begin abusing her.

"That's very sad," said Kate. "You left the relationship, though?"

"Yeah. I had to. I took Maddy one night and got – got out. Mandy helped me. She came and met us and took us to the hostel."

"Was that the Mission?"

Claudia shook her head. "No, a woman's refuge. We couldn't stay there for long, though. I used to take Maddy to a church toddler group, and I met Father Michael there. He told me there were mother and baby rooms at the Mission, and I managed to get one, after a while."

"How long have you been at the Mission?"

"Not long. Only a few months."

"But you like living there?"

Claudia shrugged. "Yeah, it's all right. I've got my name down for a council flat, but I dunno how long that's going to take."

Olbeck shifted again in his seat, easing the ache in his neck from twisting around to talk to Claudia.

"So Mandy was a kind girl, Claudia?"

"Yeah. Yeah, she was, as long as she weren't on the drugs. Then she were a right bitch." The girl coloured a little. "Sorry. It's just that – well – I knew she'd started using again just recently."

"How did you know?"

"I could tell. Also she started stealing again. She stole a silver locket that me mum had given me for Madison."

"That must have been very – hurtful," said Olbeck. "Were you angry with her?"

Claudia gave him the boldest look she'd managed so far.

"Yeah, of course."

"Did you argue?"

"Sort of. I didn't get a chance to say much. She just slammed out, and I didn't see her again."

Claudia's words seemed to strike her, and Kate saw her eyes become shiny with tears.

"I didn't see her again," repeated Claudia, softly.

"I'm sorry for your loss," said Kate, automatically. Claudia nodded silently, blinking.

"Did Mandy have a boyfriend that you know of, Claudia?"

Claudia shook her head.

"I don't think so. She never mentioned anyone."

"Did you ever see her with a man or – or a boy? Did anyone ever come to visit her that you know of?"

"No," said Claudia. She was shifting a little in her seat. Then she pulled out her phone and checked the time.

"I'm really sorry, but I've got to get Madison now."

"Right, that's fine," said Olbeck. As Claudia went to open the back door, he recalled something else.

"Claudia, one more quick thing. Did Mandy have a handbag that she used?"

"A *handbag*?" asked Claudia, and Kate was reminded of the line by Lady Bracknell in *The Importance of Being Ernest*. She tried not to grin. God knows, it wasn't funny in this context.

"What d'you mean?" asked Claudia. "Yeah, she had one, just one. She used it all the time."

"What did it look like?"

Claudia indicated her own bag.

"Like this. We got 'em together except Mandy's was white."

"Just like yours?" Kate checked. Claudia nodded. Kate quickly grabbed her phone and took a photo of Claudia's bag. Claudia didn't protest but looked a little startled.

"Thanks, Claudia. Here are our cards, if you think of anything else, please let us know."

Claudia didn't say goodbye. She ducked her head in shy, silent acknowledgement and got out of the car, closing the door quietly.

Chapter Five

DURING THAT EVENING'S RUNNING SESSION, Kate was forced, reluctantly, to admit to herself that it was getting easier. *Slightly* easier. Her face was still flushed a fetching shade of beetroot, and her t-shirt was still welded to her back with sweat, but even she couldn't deny that the actual running was getting easier. She was able to push herself a little further and run a little faster without feeling like her lungs were about to spontaneously combust inside her.

She didn't mention that to Olbeck. She'd never hear the end of it.

They finished their run along a section of the canal path, actually passing close to where Mandy Renkin had met her killer. Kate glanced at the derelict buildings as they jogged past.

"Why would she meet a punter here?" she asked, between puffs of breath. "It looks so dangerous. So dingy and dirty. Why go here?"

Olbeck was running along freely and easily.

"It's private," he said. "It's quiet, it's overlooked. Easy to do the business there if you didn't have anywhere else to go."

"Are you talking about Mandy or the perp?"

Olbeck eased down to a fast walk, and Kate followed him gratefully.

"I don't know," he said. "Surely that would apply to both of them."

"Well, exactly," said Kate, also noting that she was getting her breath back much more quickly these days. "We need to find out what Mandy's usual method of operation was. Did she normally work the streets? Had she been to this place before with punters?"

Olbeck nodded, swiping the sweatband strapped around his wrist across his glistening forehead.

"Why don't we try and track down some of her old associates? Find out whether she used to work with another girl, stuff like that."

Kate was walking normally now. She pushed some loose strands of hair off her hot face.

"Of course, there's another possibility," she said. She looked up at Olbeck and raised her eyebrows. "That she went there because she was with someone that she knew. Someone she didn't think would harm her."

Olbeck slowed. "Yes," he said slowly. "That's a possibility. That she went there with a friend or an old acquaintance."

"For sex?"

"I don't know. Who knows?"

"There didn't seem to have been any partner on the cards. Not according to Claudia."

"That's not to say there wasn't. Maybe Mandy was keeping it quiet."

"Why?"

They'd reached the end of Olbeck's street by now. Kate could see the golden lamplight shining out from the living room windows of his house, warm and friendly-looking. *I wish I had that at my place*, she thought wistfully. *Someone waiting for me at home.*

"Why would Mandy keep it quiet? I don't know. Maybe she was in a relationship with someone who was embarrassed or ashamed of her. Maybe she wasn't in a relationship at all. Oh, I don't know." Olbeck sounded irritated for a second. "We don't seem to be getting very far, do we?"

Kate shrugged.

"Let's leave it for now. We'll talk about it tomorrow."

"Kate!" exclaimed Jeff as he opened the front door. "Don't you look wonderful? Come in, darling."

"You're such a liar," said Kate, grinning and stepping forward into the hallway. "I look like a sweaty tomato."

"That's my *favourite* look," said Jeff.

"He's not lying, it actually is," said Olbeck,

receiving a kiss from his partner, which made Kate slightly uncomfortable to witness. The awkwardness only lasted a moment. Jeff swept Kate into the kitchen, where the French doors were open to the garden and a table was laid for dinner outside.

"Why don't you grab a shower while I finish dinner?" suggested Jeff. "You know where the towels are."

"I don't have anything to change into."

"Borrow one of my t-shirts," said Olbeck. "Want a drink to take up with you?"

"Okay and yes," said Kate, accepting the cool glass of orange juice, beaded with condensation. She headed upstairs and locked the bathroom door, remembering that their shower was one that started off icy and rapidly became too hot without some judicious juggling of the controls. When she'd got it to an acceptable temperature, she stripped off her clothes and hopped in.

The bathroom was pretty clean and nicely decorated, but it had enough of a homely kind of clutter to feel very lived-in. *All they need is a couple of kids, and they'd be the perfect family,* Kate thought as she sluiced herself down. She was suddenly swamped with a wave of loneliness so severe that tears sprang to her eyes. She pinched the bridge of her nose hard, leaning back against the comforting spray of hot water.

Fifteen minutes later, she'd successfully washed

the grime from her workout—and her emotions—down the drain.

"Better?" said Olbeck as she came back into the kitchen, dressed in the old Rolling Stones t-shirt he'd left hanging on the doorknob of the bathroom door for her.

"Much," said Kate, emotions under control again. She accepted a refill of her glass and stretched her clean feet out on the decking. It was still very warm, the kind of warm night rarely experienced even at the height of a British summer. Olbeck lit a citronella candle to keep away the insects.

Jeff surpassed himself with the food. It was the typical fare: healthy, heavy on the vegetables and light on lean protein, but still intensely flavourful. The first course consisted of rice-paper spring rolls accompanied by little white bowls filled with soy sauce for dipping. When these were disposed of, Jeff brought out an Asian salad, bright with slivers of carrot, red pepper and spring onion, with thin ribbons of rare beef curled like moist, pink ribbons amongst the greenery.

"God, this is delicious," said Kate, trying to eat daintily although she felt like inhaling the plateful whole. "You're such a good cook, Jeff."

"I'm a man of many talents."

That remark resulted in a sly exchange of smiles between the two men. Kate, well-aware of the innuendo, kept her eyes on her plate, eating steadily. *What's the matter with me?* She never normally minded Olbeck and Jeff being all lovey-dovey. Despite the good food and the familiar company, despite the afterglow of the exercise and the beautiful night, Kate felt itchy and cross and miserable. She had to work hard not to show it. *Probably hormones*, she told herself. *Just my luck.*

When she got home that night, the house felt very big and empty. Kate walked around, checking the doors were locked and windows tightly shut. She watched television in a desultory manner for five minutes before pressing the off button on the remote irritably. Her mobile pinged and she read a casual, chatty text from her brother Jay which, somehow, she just didn't feel like answering right away. Kate picked up a book she'd been meaning to read for several weeks, opened the cover, scanned the first page and snapped it shut again. She switched on the kettle to boil the water for her camomile tea, waiting for it to steam itself to a stop while she looked out the back kitchen window onto the darkness of the back garden. Occasionally a neighbourhood fox trotted across the lawn, but he wasn't around tonight. Kate made her tea.

Balancing her delicate cup on its saucer – tea made in a big mug just tasted wrong to her – she stood for a moment at the big, bay window in the living room, having snapped off the overhead light.

She watched the silent street outside, blinking through a veil of steam. *He's out there somewhere*, she thought, and turned abruptly away, wincing as she spilled a little hot tea over her thumb.

Safely tucked up in bed, she paged through the stored numbers in her phone, looking for the one right at the start of the list. Anderton's name glowed from the screen. Kate looked it for a moment, her thumb hovering over the call button. Then she sighed, put the phone down on her bedside table and turned out the light, lying down and drawing the duvet cover up to her chin.

J's diary

MY MOST PRESSING PROBLEM WAS, of course, what to do with the body. I'm not one of these people who do what they do to have a corpse to play with. The thought makes me feel ill. What I seek is the moment of transformation – the sinking of the knife into warm, living flesh. Once that moment has passed, there's nothing left for me there. The body is just something cumbersome and unpleasant to be disposed of as quickly as possible.

After the first blind panic had passed, I realised that I had to get rid of the body. I may not have many visitors, but I do have *some*, and there was no way I could explain away the presence of a dead tart on my kitchen floor. Not for a moment! So something had to be done. Should I dump the body? Would I get away with it? I thought uneasily of DNA, of dropped hairs and clothing fibres all leading a trail back to me. If the body was found, then I would eventually be found out. Surely?

For a few hours, I thought of all kinds of

ridiculous plans for disposing the body. Dropping it in front of a truck from a motorway bridge. Weighting it down and sinking it to the bottom of a deep lake. I knew that these fantasies were a way of getting through the horror of what I had to do. Of course in the end, I realised that the body had to stay here, in the house – or in the garden.

I thought for a while of dismembering it, but to be honest, that was beyond me, even if I had enough knowledge, dexterity and strength to actually do it. Just the thought of saws and axes chopping through bone and gristle actually made me retch. In the end, I wrapped the body up in several layers of thick plastic, taped it up and took it down to the cellar.

These old houses all have cellars. Those which have been renovated usually turn the dank, cobweb-hung, dark little rooms under the earth into modish studies, guest bedrooms, or perhaps a home cinema. Of course, Mother would never have countenanced anything like that.

Our cellar – my cellar – was as it probably had been when the house was built over a hundred years ago. The floor was brick, but right at the back, there was a boarded up aperture that was originally intended to house coal. The door in the planks at the front wasn't very big, but I was pretty sure I could get the body through intact. When I took a torch down to have a proper look, I could see the brick floor hadn't extended into the coal store – the ground was bare earth. *No wonder this house is so cold*, I thought to myself irrelevantly, before pushing myself through the little door of the coal store and gingerly standing up. I couldn't stand upright, and that presented a problem. How was I going to be able to wield a spade? I needed a deep hole.

One thing about me is that I won't give up. That used to be one of the insults flung at me by Mother, one of the many. *Stubborn as a mule, selfish, it's all about you, you, you...* Of course, the real root of the issue was that I was me and not Father, that for some reason, she'd been left with me instead of him. *Why can't you be more like your Father?* It was a constant refrain. In the end, I rather prided myself on being different to him, or I told myself that's what I felt.

So, even though burying the body in the coal store would be a tough and laborious task, it was one I set for myself and of course I completed it – eventually. I spent an hour or so every spare evening over the course of several weeks digging away with a short spade and hand trowel. Luckily, the cellar also contained a large chest freezer, and I was able to store the body in there while I prepared its final resting place.

Finally it was ready, and I levered the stiff corpse from its temporary icy tomb and transferred it to the hole dug beyond the coal store door. Once it was covered with a foot of earth, the coal door padlocked and the cellar door bolted, I toasted myself with the last of Father's whisky, raising a glass to a job well done.

For a good while after the killing, I was in what I now see as an exalted state. At first it was fuelled by the feverish grip of fear that I would be caught, but once this had abated, I felt something different but equally as intense. Everything about life seemed brighter. My usual dreary routine – work, household duties, watching television – all this seemed saturated with colour and emotion, sparkling with vivacity. I felt everything intensely. It was like being born anew, and it was an experience that I could never have anticipated. From the moment I thrust that knife into her stomach, everything had changed. I went about my day with a gladdened heart and a mind that was suddenly alive to the possibilities of the world.

And then, much as the fear had done, my acute euphoria began to ebb. Daily, little by little, this marvellous new feeling faded until the glitter and sparkle that had been mine was gone, the shine rubbed off by time and reality. I could feel the greyness gathering again, and my mood dipped and dipped and dipped until everything was back to how it had been before.

That was when I knew I had to do it again.

Chapter Six

THE NEXT MORNING, THE TEAM assembled in Anderton's office for a debrief. Kate had managed to grab a chair, but after seeing Theo hobble in on his crutches, she stood up again and made him take it. He collapsed onto it and stuck his plastered foot out carefully, giving her a grateful smile.

Anderton spun on his heel, realised how close he was to the wall and spun back again, thwarted.

"*When* do we move back?" he implored. "This is intolerable."

"Next Monday," said Jane, confidently. "I've just had an email from the Facilities Team. We're back in on Monday."

"Thank God for that. We'll have to have champagne. Now, where were we?"

"Stuffed into your office," said Olbeck with a grin.

"Very funny, Mark. How are we getting on with Mandy Renkin?"

Olbeck immediately became serious. "Kate and

I have interviewed her friend, the priest who runs the Mission that provided her accommodation and one of the volunteers who works at the Mission."

"Get anything?"

Olbeck hesitated for a moment. Kate took up the baton.

"It seems quite likely that Mandy had gone back to using drugs. That could well be why she taken up prostitution again – to get the money."

Anderton nodded. "We'll have the tests back from the path lab this week. Should be easy enough to see whether that was the case. Now, it's a possibility that it's a drug-related crime, although I'm inclined to think that it's not. It's an angle worth investigating, though. Go through the records, see if we have any dealers we can lean on. Anyone with a record of violent crime, knife crime, that sort of thing. Rav, you do that."

He swung around, churning his hair with both hands. "What else? No one's mentioned a partner, a boyfriend. Was there one?"

There was silence from the team. Anderton lowered his hands and his gaze swept the room.

"You need to start doing some more questioning. Kate, Mark, go back to the Mission, talk to Father Whatshisname again. Get some more background."

"Fine," said Kate. "But we're interviewing the social worker today and the foster family."

Anderton raised his eyebrows.

"Okay, good stuff. Do a follow up at the Mission when you can. Okay team, unless anyone else has anything to add, let's get on."

No one had anything to add. They began to file slowly out. Kate, one of the last to leave except Theo, saw Anderton walk over to him and say something in a low tone, speaking too quietly for Kate to hear.

She lingered outside the office until Theo hobbled out on his crutches, and they walked back to the temporary office together.

"What did Anderton want?" asked Kate unblushingly.

Theo was by necessity looking at the floor as he swung himself along.

"What?"

"What did he say to you at the end?"

Theo looked up and grinned.

"Nosy. Nothing much. He just asked me to check the national databases for similar cases."

Kate frowned. "Similar?"

"Yeah. Similar weapon, similar MO." They reached the door of the office, and Kate hurried to hold it open for Theo. "Thanks. Anyway, that's all he wanted. Why?"

"No reason," said Kate, rather absently. She was thinking.

"You can do it if you want. He's only getting me to do it 'cos I'm stuck behind a desk at the moment."

"I wouldn't want to deprive you," said Kate,

grinning. "Let me know if you do find anything though, okay?"

They parted at the entrance to the office, and Kate went to sit down at her desk. The instant her backside made contact with the chair, she sprung up again and hurried back to Anderton's office. The door was shut, but she knocked anyway and was rewarded with an interrogative 'Yup?' from inside.

"Kate," said Anderton as she closed the door behind her. He looked surprised. "What's wrong?"

"Nothing's wrong," she answered. "I just wanted to ask you something."

"Uh-huh. What's that?"

"Why did you ask Theo to cross-check for similar cases?"

Anderton sat back in his chair. Slowly, he laced the fingers of both hands behind his neck and rocked back a little.

"Why do you ask?" he said after a moment.

Kate smiled.

"I asked first."

Anderton grinned. "There's no secret. I want to check whether there have been any other cases like this one."

"Why?"

His eyebrows rose. "Why? Why do you think? So we can find the person who did it, of course."

Kate shook her head, flustered.

"I didn't mean why, I meant—" She stopped

herself for a moment. Then she took a deep breath and asked the question she really wanted the answer to.

"You don't think this is just a one off, do you, sir? I mean, you think there are going to be more."

Anderton took his hands down from behind his neck. He leaned forward, fixing Kate with his stare.

"Now, why would you say that?" he asked.

Kate kept her eyes on his but she shrugged.

"I don't know," she said after a moment. "Call it a feeling."

Anderton was silent for a moment.

"You scare me sometimes, Kate," he said. "I'll have to hide my thoughts from you from now on, God knows how."

Kate smiled.

"That depends on what they are."

She'd meant it to be a light-hearted response, but their eyes locked again, and she was shocked at the sudden rush of heat that went through her. She shifted a little in her chair, her gaze dropping.

Anderton cleared his throat.

"You're right," he said. "I have a bad feeling about this case. And *I* can't say how I know that. Call it a feeling."

There was a moment's silence. Anderton sat back in his seat again.

"Don't mention this to the rest of the team,

okay? I could be wrong. I *hope* I'm wrong. Let's see how things – pan out."

Kate nodded. She had been intently focused on the case, but now her thoughts were swirling around something very different. She stood up and said goodbye, casually, just as if she wasn't thinking about jumping over the desk to throw herself into Anderton's arms.

Back at her desk, she stared blankly at the screen, barely aware of the bustle and activity going on around her. Then she closed her eyes. The intensity of her feelings shocked her. How was she going to keep her mind on the case? She suddenly became aware that Olbeck was stood behind her, repeating himself impatiently for what was obviously not the first time.

"What?"

"I said, what did you ask Anderton about?"

"Nothing," said Kate. Olbeck gave her an old-fashioned look.

"Seriously," she added. "I'll tell you later." She made a massive effort to stop thinking pornographic thoughts about her boss and turned her attention back to work. "What are we doing now?"

"Mandy Renkin's social worker," said Olbeck. "I've already made an appointment with her. Come on, you can drive, seeing as you're so keen on it."

Barbara Fee was a thin, harassed-looking woman, much wound about with scarves and with fine, flyaway hair messily pinned up in an unsuccessful chignon. Whole hanks of hair kept escaping, and Ms Fee would shove them back in with a distracted air. She received Kate and Olbeck in her chaotic office with the proviso that she 'really only had twenty minutes' before her next appointment.

"We'll be as quick as we can then," said Kate. "What can you tell us about Mandy Renkin?"

Barbara Fee pushed at a slipping hairslide.

"She was a nice girl," she said. "Had problems, obviously. Usual story: taken into care at an early age, in and out of the care system, drug problems, teen pregnancy, had her child taken away from her. What else did you want to know?"

"Was she ever fostered?" asked Kate. "I found a school prize that she must have received when she was about fourteen. She was obviously doing well at school then. That doesn't really tally with her later...life, shall we say."

Barbara Fee was hunting amongst the files of her messy desk.

"No, you're right," she said, rather absently. She found what she was looking for and offered it across the table to Olbeck, who took the thick manila folder. "That's her file. She *was* fostered, from the age of ten to the age of fifteen. Settled pretty nicely, actually. The family was one who tended to take on older children and teenagers, very experienced foster carers. Mandy did very well with them."

Olbeck was leafing through the file.

"So, what happened?" he asked. "Why did she go off the rails?"

Barbara tucked a loose strand of hair behind one ear.

"Teenage rebellion?" she said. "Unresolved issues with the breakdown of her family unit? She got in with the wrong crowd? Take your pick. You can only do so much for these kids, you know. At some point, you just have to take a step back and realise you're doing more harm than good."

"Could you give us the address of her foster parents?"

"Yes, of course. They're still fostering for us. Bernard and Adele Watkins." Barbara Fee handed over a scrap of paper with an address scribbled on it. "Terrible thing to happen to Mandy, but she wouldn't be the first. They live such dangerous lives, these girls. They're so vulnerable."

"Did you like Mandy?" asked Kate as they were ushered from the office.

Barbara stared at her.

"Like her? What do you mean? She was a nice girl, like I said."

"No, I meant did you *like* her?" asked Kate. "As a person?"

Barbara was rummaging in her bag for her keys.

She withdrew a set that had to have had twenty keys on one inadequate key ring and locked her office door.

"Yes, of course," she said, vaguely. "Now, I really must go, if you'll excuse me."

They watched her walk away down the long corridor, the cork heels of her Birkenstock sandals slapping loudly against the tiled floor like ironic applause following her exit.

J's Diary

I'VE BEEN THINKING A LOT about Mother lately. It's annoying, because I thought I'd successfully managed to forget her, often for whole hours at a time. Oddly, it's not the old Mother that I think about, the white-haired, bespectacled, bent old lady who shuffled around the house. The weak one, the one who finally found out that a sharp tongue is no real defence. No, it's the Mother from a time I never knew that I find myself thinking about, the Mother of the photographs from the war and post-war: the dark-haired, slim and pretty Mother in her tea dresses and Victory rolls. The Mother who met my father.

My father has been a ghost in my life, always. Never physically here but always a shadowy presence in the house. He was never allowed to rest, never allowed to fade away into oblivion, like so many other of the men who never made it home from the war. Mother kept him alive, in her memory, in her conversation, in the photographs that littered the house. I think I was about thirteen when I realised the ratio of pictures of Father to me: one of me to every twenty of him. All of mine were baby pictures – I think the oldest one was of me as a three-year-old, dressed in muddy dungarees. In one of baby pictures, I'm sat on the hearth rug, waving a blurred object that I think is a rattle and wearing a blue-striped sailor suit.

The picture that takes pride of place in the living room is on the mantelpiece in an enormous gilt frame. It's a sepia-toned shot of my mother and father on their wedding day, 15th July 1940, my father in his uniform, my mother in blue silk. I know she wore blue because she told me – in the picture, her dress is a nothingy-brown colour. They were married two weeks before he was posted overseas, long enough for him to impregnate her with what turned out to be me. He never came back.

I don't know why I keep maundering on about the past. Perhaps it's because I'm getting older myself, and it necessarily preys more on my mind. It's the future I should be thinking of. The next girl, and the next one after that. If I am going to write about the past, I should write about the second girl and how it turned out to be as wonderful as the first.

Mother always accused me of being irrational, of having no self-control. She was wrong about that, just as she was about so many things. When I decide on a course of action, I always go through with it. I make my plans and set out my stall; step by careful step, I achieve what I want. When I decided I wanted to repeat what I'd done with the first girl, I spent weeks thinking about it, considering how to do it and get away with it, as I had so cleverly the first time. In some ways, the anticipation made things even better.

Much as it was convenient, having the tart come to my home, it just wasn't feasible or practical. For one thing, someone was bound to notice my visitor at some point, and for another, I couldn't continue to store the bodies at home. The coal hole would only hold one more at most, and there was no way I was going to start digging in the garden. I have never been a gardener, and since Mother died, all I have done is cut the lawn. If I started digging a huge trench in the back flowerbeds, someone would be bound to become suspicious.

But if I couldn't bring her here, where could I go? To visit a brothel was out of the question – I would be found out in a matter of minutes. I thought, momentarily, of hiring an anonymous room somewhere using a false name and paying with cash, but that was fraught with danger. I could be so easily traced.

I have to admit, I was stumped for several days. My predicament made me snappy and irritable, but luckily, people at work and the neighbours I met in the street put my bad temper down to grief over my recent bereavement. It was about the only time Mother was ever of use to me.

Eventually I decided I would go far away, to a small town with a thriving red light district. I would scope out possible sites where I would not be discovered, where I would be overlooked. Then I would find myself someone suitable, meet her at my chosen spot, and then...

I need to keep writing about the second girl but for some reason I find myself wanting to write about Mother. If I ever had to talk to someone about Mother – not that I ever would, or did – I think I would find it hard to explain exactly how she used to keep control of me, keep me cowed and shivering like a whipped dog. To this day, I don't know how she managed it.

There were only a few beatings, or perhaps it's more accurate to say that there were only a few that I can remember. One particularly painful one sticks in my memory because I remember focusing on the brooch she was wearing at the time. She had many brooches, and this one was in the shape of a butterfly, in a shade that recalled the summer sky at noon: a hard, pitiless blue. As the blows rained down, making my ears ring and my eyes squint down to slits, as I tried to absorb the jolts to my head and shoulders, all I could see was that butterfly shape. I think it was the last thing I remember seeing before I lost consciousness.

I think that was the last proper beating Mother gave me. I don't know, but I'm guessing that I was unconscious for a long time, and perhaps she thought she'd done some real damage. Perhaps she'd thought she'd killed me. Knowing her, it wouldn't have been anticipated grief for her dead child that stopped her doing it again. No, it would be the fact that everyone would find out, that everyone would finally realise the kind of person she really was.

It's no wonder, really, that I ended up the kind of person that I am. I learned it all from Mother: how to hide your real identity, how to put on a mask that fools the rest of the world. Only you know, deep inside, who you really are.

Chapter Seven

KATE WENT BACK TO THE Mission building the next morning, having rung ahead to check that Claudia was in residence. Margaret Paling was not in the reception booth this time; another woman, also grey-haired, also elderly, peered at Kate's warrant card suspiciously and let her through the security door to the lounge beyond.

Kate knocked on Claudia's door. A few moments later, it was flung wide by Claudia, who had a beaming smile on her face – a smile that cooled and died when she saw Kate.

"Good morning," said Kate, stepping forward across the threshold. "Were you expecting someone?"

Claudia muttered something, a possible negative, but Kate couldn't quite hear. The room was much larger than Mandy's, with two single beds against opposite walls, a large wardrobe, chest of drawers and, most significantly, a small girl with a mop of dark hair and large, dark eyes who was sat on the floor surrounded by toys and regarding Kate with a frown.

Kate cursed inwardly. Why hadn't she realised Claudia's daughter would be here? It was going to be almost impossible to talk about anything to do with the case in front of a small child. She thought quickly.

"I need to ask you a few more questions about Mandy, Claudia," she said. "Is there anyone who could look after Madison while we have a talk?"

Claudia shook her head, nervously.

"There's no one I'd leave her with here," she said. The little girl got up and pressed herself to the side of her mother, twining her thin little arms around Claudia's leg.

"No, okay," said Kate. "Why don't we all go for a walk? Madison, is there a playground near here you'd like to go to?"

There turned out to be a small patch of recreational ground with a couple of battered swings and a chipped and rusting climbing frame about five minutes' walk from the Mission. Madison clambered around the structure while her mother watched, and Kate tried to think of the questions she needed to ask. She was distracted by the thought that – given a different choice back in her teens – this could have been *her* life, trying to raise a child alone with no money and little support, trapped in a low-paying job if she was lucky and on benefits if she wasn't. *This could have been me.*

Kate suddenly and quite fervently knew that she *had* made the right choice back when she was seventeen. As hard as it had been at the time and for years afterwards. As hard as it sometimes still was. She'd made the right choice.

She made a massive effort to bring her mind back to the job. Claudia hadn't noticed her period of silence; she was watching Madison swinging herself back and forth with a proud, tender look on her face.

"Madison's a lovely little girl," said Kate, and she was rewarded by Claudia's pleased smile.

"She's a little monkey," said Claudia in the most animated tone Kate had yet heard from her.

"Mandy had a child, didn't she?"

Claudia's face clouded.

"Yeah," she said after a moment. "But he got took off of her by the social. She couldn't look after him properly. She was doing too many drugs at the time. It broke her heart when he went."

"I know I've asked you this before, Claudia, but are you sure that Mandy didn't have a boyfriend?"

Claudia still had her eyes fixed on Madison, who was trying to climb the frame of the swing and sliding down again. She shrugged.

"I told you, I dunno. I don't think so."

"Would she have told you if she had?"

"She might have. But I don't think she was seeing anyone. She always said men were bad news."

Kate nodded.

"How about you, Claudia?"

Startled, Claudia looked at her.

"What d'you mean?"

"Do you have someone? A boyfriend or partner? It must be hard raising a child by yourself."

Kate was only really making conversation, not really interested in the answer. A rising tide of blood suffused Claudia's face, and Kate regretted her casual words.

"No," said Claudia, after a moment. "I don't have no one."

Me neither, agreed Kate silently. *Me neither*.

"I FEEL LIKE I SHOULD be cutting a ribbon or something," said Anderton, one hand on the door to the renovated room. He flung it open with a flourish. "Ta-da!"

The team crowded in behind him, reacting with varying degrees of enthusiasm. Jane and Kate made appropriate 'oohs,' Olbeck, Theo and Rav nodded their cautious assent and Jerry lowered his brows and said something very similar to 'humph.'

"Well," said Anderton. "We're back in at least, thank God. I said something like this calls for champagne, didn't I?"

"You definitely said that," said Olbeck.

"Well, you'll find I'm a man of my word. We'll all have a little celebratory drink later."

This statement was met with a rather more enthusiastic response. The team sat down to their desks and applied themselves to their work with renewed energy. Kate rolled her chair back and forth over the new laminate and spun around a little, taking in the fresh new paint and the new skylights, which brought in the bright mid-summer sun.

She became aware that Theo was waving at her from the other side of the room.

"What's up?" she asked, making her way over to him.

He beckoned her down to his seated level.

"You know how you asked me about whether I'd found anything that resembled the MO? Similar murder weapon, situation, et cetera et cetera?"

"Yes," said Kate, alert now. She grabbed a spare chair and sat down next to Theo.

"Well, I've found one."

"Seriously?" Kate bent lower, looking at his computer screen. She lowered her voice. "Have you told Anderton yet?"

"Not yet."

"But you're telling me first?"

Theo grinned. "I'm nice like that. Also, you're subbing me in the run."

"Oh, that."

"Yeah, so I owe you. Anyway, look here." He tapped keys and brought up one of the database screens. "Murder of a prostitute in Brighton. Ingrid Davislova, age twenty-two years. Originally from Poland. She'd only been here a year or so, poor cow."

Kate read the rest of the details. The victim had been short, slim, dark-haired, and the murder weapon, which hadn't been found, was estimated to be some sort of serrated kitchen knife.

"This was just under eight months ago." She ran her eyes over the words and numbers on the screen once more. "It's good, Theo. It sounds like it could be our guy."

"I'm going to tell the boss. Give us a hand up, will you?"

Kate helped him up and balanced him while he tucked the crutches under his arms.

"Shall I tell him you know already?" asked Theo, stuffing the papers under one arm and wobbling a little as he attempted to turn around.

Kate shook her head.

"Not yet," she said. "Not just yet."

Kate's task for the afternoon was to interview Mandy Renkin's foster parents. Adele Watkins opened the front door of the Victorian-terraced house. She was a massive woman, not tall, but very overweight, with a fat, still-pretty face and short, curly grey hair. Clearly unembarrassed by her size, Adele wore loose trousers and a tunic in jewel-bright colours, and her chubby fingers sparkled with rings. Kate warmed to her immediately.

The house was very cluttered, the furniture was battered and the carpets were worn, but there was still an air of homely comfort throughout. A greyhound, as thin as its owner was fat, was curled in a dog basket in the messy kitchen, its sharp, bony muzzle resting on the side of the basket. Liquid brown eyes followed Kate as she walked past to the chair that Adele indicated at the table, and the dog's whip-like tail thumped. It whimpered softly.

"All right, you old softy," said Adele, and the dog jumped up immediately and came over to Kate, wiggling its bottom like a Caribbean dancer. Kate, charmed, stroked the head that had been laid in her lap as she listened to Adele talk about Mandy.

"Nice girl, lovely girl. Kind and intelligent. Too intelligent for her own good, I always thought. She had a tragic history. Well, my dear, they all do, to be honest."

"Have you fostered many children, Mrs Watkins?"

"Seems like hundreds. It's not, of course, but I've been doing this for – oh, twenty years now. I couldn't have any of my own. That's what got me started."

"I'm sorry to hear that," said Kate, automatically.

She pulled the dog's silky ears gently, and it gave a whimper of pleasure.

"Well, perhaps it was for the best," said Adele. "I've been able to help a lot of children over the years, and if I'd had my own, well who knows whether I would have fostered any? No, I can't complain. I feel we've had a family, Bernard and I. It's very satisfying to know that you're able to give a child a stable home. There's so many kids out there who need one."

"Barbara Fee said as much. She said Mandy settled here really well."

"She did. She was a bit younger than the ones we usually have. We make a point of having the teenagers here if they need a place."

"Why is that?"

Adele pushed a plate of biscuits over to her. "Well, no one else wants them, my dear, you see? Most foster carers, most people who adopt – they want the babies, don't they? The littlies."

Kate flinched, unable to help herself. When would that ever stop hurting? She coughed, keeping her face as blank as she could.

Adele didn't seem to have noticed her momentary wince. She was looking out the kitchen window at a garden filled with a trampoline, a rusting swing and several bikes leaning up against the wall of a shed.

"Mandy had been in and out of care homes since she was five. She was desperate for a real home, somewhere where she could feel like she was in a family."

"Did she have any contact with her birth family at all?"

"No. No she didn't. Her mother was a chronic alcoholic. She's dead now, poor woman. I think she actually had Mandy put up for adoption, though. I mean, rather than Mandy being removed from her care."

Kate was careful to keep her voice steady when she asked the next question.

"How old was Mandy when that happened?"

Adele ran chubby fingers through her grey curls.

"I'm not sure, my dear, to be honest. It was such a long time ago now. I think she was two – two, maybe three?"

"And Mandy went into care? She wasn't adopted?"

"No, unfortunately not. No, they couldn't find a placement for her."

Kate scratched at the dog's ears, and it whined again with pleasure.

"That's sad," she murmured.

"Yes," said Adele, briefly. "It's amazing that she was as bright and as – well – normal as she could be by the time she came to us. Still, it took its toll though, those years in care. Yes, it took its toll."

"So Mandy came to you when she was ten?"

Adele nodded. "She settled immediately. Did

well at school, made friends. We even thought she might go onto university."

"So what happened?"

Adele Watkins sighed. She eased her bulk a little in the slightly too-small kitchen chair.

"Oh, my dear," she said. "I could tell you that it was her boyfriend's fault. That would be the obvious explanation."

"Would this be Mike Fenton you're talking about?"

"Mike, yes – that was his name." Adele fell silent for a moment. Then she heaved herself off of her chair and went over to the kitchen dresser, crammed with crockery, cookery books, plastic toys, a child's sock, an empty beer bottle, a blackening banana and other assorted household detritus. From the chaos she extracted a small, framed photograph and handed it to Kate.

Kate looked at the picture. A teenage girl, bright-faced and smiling, dressed in her school uniform, with a slightly crooked fringe and freckles. Kate thought of that copy of *Great Expectations* in Mandy's room, the inscription on the flyer. Then she saw Mandy's dead face on Doctor Telling's examination table. She felt her fingers clench on the wooden frame.

"She was lovely," she said in a low voice.

Adele sat down again, heavily.

"She was. It's not—"

For a moment, her voice cracked. She turned her head sharply away from Kate to look again out of the window as if the view of the suburban garden fascinated her.

"It's not fair," said Adele after a moment. She cleared her throat. "Life's not fair though, is it, my dear?"

Kate said nothing but handed her back the picture, gently. Adele took it and propped it up against the vase of flowers that stood in the middle of the kitchen table.

"So, Mike Fenton is the one you blame?" asked Kate.

Adele looked at her with a gentle smile.

"No, I said that would be the obvious explanation. He was the one who introduced her to drugs after all. But no, I don't really blame him. Mandy made her own choices. She just made bad ones because she was missing something, you see."

"Missing something?"

Adele picked up the photograph again, regarding the bright, pretty face of the young girl trapped within the frame.

"I don't think you can conceive of the damage it does to a child when she has the kind of upbringing – or lack of it – that Mandy had," she explained. "When your mother doesn't want you – when you know your mother didn't want you – when you're rejected from that early an age, there's a part of you that doesn't ever recover. I think, somewhere deep down, you're always aware of the *lack*, you know. There's always a part of you that's missing."

There was a long moment of silence. Adele looked up at Kate.

"I'm sorry, my dear, are you all right?"

"I'm fine," said Kate with a clenched and frozen smile. "Thank you for seeing me, Mrs Watkins. You've been very helpful."

Adele looked a little surprised but heaved herself to her feet.

"Any time, my dear. I hope I've been of some help."

"Very much so," said Kate. She shook hands on the doorstep and handed over her card. "Thank you very much."

"Goodbye."

Kate made herself lift a hand in farewell as she reached the garden gate. Then she hurried around the corner, out of sight, and burst into tears.

Chapter Eight

"ALL RIGHT, ALL RIGHT," SAID Anderton. "I can see you're all eagerly eyeing up the booze behind me. Before we get stuck in, I want a quick rundown of where we're at. Who wants to start?"

They were all gathered in the once-pristine office, which was rapidly returning to its usual state of messiness. Behind Anderton's pacing figure stood a table with four bottles of champagne and a variety of glasses ranging from champagne flutes, a novelty shot glass from Ibiza and a beer mug. *Real* champagne too, not cheap fizz.

"Anybody?" asked Anderton.

Kate waved her hand.

"I interviewed Mandy's foster mother this afternoon. Mandy lived with the family for about five years until she left home to live with her boyfriend."

"Would this be the junkie one? Mark Fenton?"

"Mike Fenton, sir. Yes, that's the one."

Anderton propped himself against the table, causing the bottles to chink against one another.

"Whoops."

"Don't spill it," said Olbeck, grinning.

"God forbid. Anyway, what about this Mike Fenton? He's the one who introduced Mandy to drugs, got her on the downward spiral. I suppose we have eliminated him from our enquiries? Anyone checked on his whereabouts?"

Jane put her hand up.

"I did, sir. Did that as soon as I had the name from Kate and Mark's interview with Claudia Smith."

Anderton looked pleased.

"You did? Quick work Jane, well done." Jane smiled a bashful, modest smile. "So, what have we got?"

"Well sir, it definitely wasn't him."

"And why is that?"

"Because he's dead. Died about four years ago."

"Aha." Anderton eased himself from the edge of the table and began walking up and down again. "Let me guess. Drugs overdose?"

Jane shook her head. "Funnily enough, no. He was killed in a car crash."

"Well, there we go. He's still dead. Not our guy. Okay, what else?" He looked keenly across the room. "Theo?"

Theo was from necessity sitting down; his plastered leg stuck out in front of him.

He smiled rather self-consciously.

"There was a case, in Brighton, that strongly resembles our case here. Same sort of murder weapon. Same type of victim. The Brighton case was unsolved."

Anderton nodded. Kate, looking around at the other faces, saw a variety of expressions: uneasiness, excitement, scepticism, eagerness. Jerry was staring out of the window, his thoughts clearly far from this room.

Anderton raised his hand as if to quell a hubbub, although there was silence in the room.

"Now, I should mention that I asked Theo to look for cases with a similar MO," he said. "Don't go leaping to any enormous conclusions or anything. It's just something I thought should be looked into, that's all."

Olbeck asked the same question Kate had asked a few days ago.

"You think there will be more, sir? Are we talking another Ipswich, or something?"

Anderton had stopped pacing. He lifted his shoulders and dropped them.

"I don't know. I have no idea. I hope—" He was silent for a second. "We're planning for the worst, that's all. I hope I'm wrong."

There was another short period of silence, more loaded than the last. Then Anderton broke it.

"Now, don't go getting all panicky. I just want

someone to follow up on the possible Brighton connection, that's all. Get a bit more info. Jerry!" Jerry almost jumped. "You've got contacts there, haven't you? Could you give one of them a ring, take a visit, that sort of thing?"

Jerry looked for a moment as if he were going to refuse. Then he shrugged.

"Okay, then. I'll go tomorrow."

"Good. Right then, if no one else has anything, I think we can call a halt to the official proceedings and prepare to declare this new office open." He turned to the table behind him and picked up the first bottle, ripping the gold foil from the top.

"Anyone got anything they want to say?"

"May God bless this new office and all who sail in her," said Olbeck, laughing.

"Quite right," said Anderton and the cork exploded from the bottle, ricocheting of the ceiling before a spume of froth shot out from the neck of the bottle, all over the new flooring. Jane shrieked and Rav whooped.

"Shit," said Anderton, grinning. "Don't just stand there, get me some glasses!"

Anderton began the slow journey around the room with a tray full of brimming glasses. He paused in front of Kate, Theo and Olbeck.

"Here you go," he said. The men took a glass each. Anderton went to leave.

"Wait," said Kate, suddenly reckless. "I'll have one."

All three men did a genuine double-take. Anderton was first to recover his composure.

"Right you are." He inclined the tray so that the biggest glass was nearest Kate's hand. "Why not? If you can't beat 'em, join 'em, eh, Kate?"

Kate took the glass and took a sip. Anderton moved on with the now-depleted tray.

Kate became aware of both Theo and Olbeck boggling at her.

"What?" she said, a little annoyed.

"Where is Kate Redman, and what have you done with her?" asked Olbeck.

"Check her pulse, she could be an alien imposter," said Theo, grinning.

"Oh, leave it out," said Kate. "I do have the odd drink, you know. I'm not *totally* teetotal. I've even got pissed with you both once."

"That was eight months ago," said Olbeck. "And you've not touched a drop since, at least that I'm aware of. What's the big occasion?"

Kate shrugged.

"Don't know. Just felt like it, I suppose."

"Well, damn it – cheers then." Olbeck clinked glasses with her, and after a second, Theo followed suit.

"You got any more on the Brighton case, Theo?" asked Kate after they'd all taken a drink. "Anything that you haven't told us?"

Theo was opening his mouth to answer when Olbeck cut across him.

"No, *no*," he said. "I absolutely forbid it. For once, we are not going to talk shop. Let's talk about something else. Anything."

"Wait while a deathly silence falls," said Kate. Then she relented. "All right, why not. Anyone seen any good films lately?"

Once the champagne ran out, the team decamped to the pub. Jane cried off, citing childcare arrangements, but everyone else headed for the battered old tavern three streets away that had almost become a second, unofficial office. Kate, Jerry and Olbeck sat down at the usual corner table next to the flashing fruit machines. Anderton and Rav headed for the bar, and Theo hobbled out to the garden for a cigarette.

Olbeck's phone rang. Answering the call, he waved an apology at Kate and Jerry and squeezed past them to take his phone call out in the relatively quiet street.

Kate and Jerry sat in an awkward silence, made somehow worse by the friendly tumult going on around them. Kate resisted the urge to check her own phone for messages. The unaccustomed champagne made her bold. Without stopping to think about whether it was a good idea or not, she turned to Jerry.

"So, why can't we be friends, Jerry? Why do we

have this awkwardness between us? Is it something I've done?"

The smaller, sober part of her was aghast. Jerry was looking at her as if she'd just got up on the table and urinated in his pint glass.

"You what?" he said after a moment.

The tone of his voice should have warned Kate off, and if she hadn't drunk the best part of a half a bottle of champagne, she would have laughed and changed the subject and possibly ran out of the pub on the flimsiest of excuses. Instead, she repeated her question.

The long moment of silence that followed was lengthy enough for Kate to begin to feel rather unpleasantly sober. Then Jerry, not taking his eyes off hers, spoke.

"Yeah, you're right," he said. "I don't like you. Why would I?"

"Why would you?" Kate was aware she was blinking rapidly and shaking her head. "What do you mean? Why – why would you feel that way?"

Jerry scoffed. He turned to look back at the beer garden, the light dimming as the long summer twilight gradually gave way to night.

"Why wouldn't I?" he said. "Why? Why would I *like*, much less *respect*, someone who gets ahead by getting on her back?"

For a frozen moment, Kate thought she'd misheard him. Anderton was making his way back to the table with another tray full of drinks, Rav bringing up the rear.

"You what?" she asked, shock mangling her grammar.

"You heard me," said Jerry. "Slag," he added, almost as an afterthought.

Kate felt her hand go out without even thinking about it. Two seconds later, the remains of her glass of wine was running down Jerry's astonished face.

"Fuck!"

There was a confused scrimmage and a loud 'hey, hey' from Olbeck, who was making his way back to the table. Kate saw Jerry's hand clench into a fist, draw back. Time seemed to slow down. She was dimly aware that her lips were drawn back over her teeth, bared like an animal's.

"What the fuck? *Jerry*—"

Olbeck had his hand in front of Jerry's wine-drenched face, blocking his arm. Anderton and Rav were at the table, crashing down the drinks. There was a loud shout of "Oy! Take it outside!" from the bar. Kate and Jerry sat glaring at each other until Anderton clamped a hand about Kate's wrist and virtually dragged her outside into the street.

"*What* the *hell*?"

Kate said nothing, but stood rubbing her wrist. She thought of telling Anderton – of all people! – what Jerry had said, what he'd accused her of. Rage and shame mounted in her chest, flooded her throat and rose until it was pricking the back of her eyes. She turned away, shaking her head.

"Where are you going?"

"Home," Kate muttered. Olbeck appeared in the pub doorway with Rav close behind him. She mouthed a 'sorry' at them and turned, beginning to walk away, not wanting to see the surprise and shock on their faces.

"Kate, for God's sake—"

Anderton appeared at her side. She turned her head away and walked a little faster. She was aware she was behaving ridiculously, but her hurt pride didn't seem to be able to let her laugh it off and apologise.

"Kate Redman, would you stop behaving like a child and listen to me for a second?"

Kate came to a halt at the end of the road, finally stopped in her path by Anderton's tone. She'd heard that voice once or twice before in her career, never in the most cheerful of circumstances. She stared across the road, seeing the passing cars and the streetlights through a smear of salt water.

"What did Jerry say to you?" asked Anderton in a gentler tone.

Kate cleared her throat.

"It doesn't matter," she said. "I'm sorry about throwing the drink."

"Don't apologise to *me*."

Kate finally turned to stare at him. He was looking at her in a way she couldn't decipher.

"Well, I'm not apologising to him," she said through clenched teeth. There was a long, charged moment as their eyes met. Then Kate turned away.

"I'm going home," she muttered.

"I'll walk you home."

"Don't bother," she retorted and then immediately regretted her rudeness. Anderton took no notice. He put a hand under her arm and escorted her across the road during a gap in the traffic.

"I *will* walk you home, DS Redman," he said. "There's a man who kills women on the loose in this town. Do you think I'm going to have you walking about after dark in a tired and emotional state while he's still around?"

They had reached the opposite pavement by this time, and Anderton removed his hand. Kate could still feel the warmth of where it had rested on the underside of her arm.

"Women?" she asked, after a moment.

"Well, a woman. Whatever the semantics are, I'm not having you walking home alone. Is that clear?"

"Yes, sir," murmured Kate. All of a sudden, she felt exhausted.

"Right, which way do we go?"

They walked in silence for several minutes.

Kate could feel the alcohol wearing off, leaving a heaviness in her limbs, an incipient headache tapping at her temples. She rubbed her hands under her eyes. What an idiot she had been. But how much of a bastard was Jerry? Seriously, what *was* his problem? Why had he accused her of – of what he had?

"Why would he *say* that?"

"What's that?"

"Oh." Kate realised she'd spoken her thought aloud. "It doesn't matter."

"Okay."

They walked on a bit further.

"Why is Jerry such a pig?" Kate burst out, unable to keep it in any longer. "Why does he have such a problem with me?"

"I don't know," said Anderton, mildly. "He's never had much time for women."

"The ignorant, sexist, stupid *pig*."

"Now, Kate," said Anderton, stepping around the remains of someone's takeaway curry on the pavement. "Sexist pig he may be, but he's certainly not stupid."

"No?"

"He went to Cambridge, for a start."

Kate snorted, sure Anderton was joking. Then she looked at him more closely.

"You're joking, right?"

"Nope. Clare College, if I remember correctly."

"*Jerry*?" Kate struggled to keep her mouth shut as she thought, *Well, what the fuck is he doing in the police force?*

"It was a long time ago."

"No kidding." How old *was* Jerry, anyway? Surely he was coming up to retirement age. Kate said as much.

"Yes, that's right," said Anderton. They were approaching Kate's street. "That's another reason I would be – making allowances for his behaviour, shall we say? He's been on the force for years and that's all he knows. I can't imagine what he'll do with himself once he retires. It's making him snappy. Irritable. That's all. Not to mention the fact that he's had a bit of a hard year."

He didn't elaborate. Kate walked on in silence for a moment, picturing Jerry; trying to reconcile the abrupt, overweight, grey-haired, uptight policeman she knew with a Cambridge university student. The stereotypical image of one, at least: black-gowned, floppy hair, upper-class accent.

"Is this you?"

Kate realised they has stopped outside her garden gate. She looked up at her house, at the dark windows, the lack of light within. Then she looked at Anderton.

"See, this is why I don't drink."

"What do you mean?"

"I do stupid things."

They were standing very close to one another. Kate could feel his breath on her face, beer-scented.

"Is that what you call it?" Anderton said. He wasn't looking in her eyes, he was looking at her mouth.

Kate could feel the precipice beneath her feet. Down there was – what? Damnation? Or salvation?

"I don't know what else you'd call this," she said, and she stepped forward into his arms.

J's diary

AFTER BRIGHTON, I FELT INVINCIBLE. It had gone even better than I'd hoped. I'd spent a few days walking around the town, disguised as myself, disguised as a tourist. I stayed in a hotel, an anonymous chain hotel, because I wanted as low a profile as possible, particularly when it came to the actual night of the killing. I was pleasant to any of the fellow guests who spoke to me, although few did, as my usual disguise is such a boring, uninteresting one. I am totally forgettable. This is both a blessing and a curse.

I would find a nice restaurant and eat my evening meal there, companioned only by my book. I would have a modest glass of wine, eat my dinner and then go back to the hotel, murmuring a 'good night' to the receptionists behind the desk. I prepared myself in my room, excitement mounting with every minute that ticked by, fortifying myself with whisky and checking and rechecking that I had the knife tucked safely inside my jacket pocket.

Then I would creep out, through the back entrance that I'd discovered on my first night there. Even if there were CCTV cameras about, my hat, scarf and glasses would provide enough camouflage.

It was on the third night that I found the perfect one: small, slim and dark-haired. I saw her emerge from a car at the side of the street that I'd already noted as a likely hunting ground. This is where the tarts worked, strutting for custom, taking their punters into the darkened wasteland that stood behind an abandoned factory. I watched from my vantage point and chose the right moment. She was looking about her as I came up to her and presented my request in a low voice. She was drunk or stoned or something; she was swaying on her feet, pupils dilated even further than they should be, even in the darkness surrounding us. There was no one else around.

She stumbled over the rough ground as we walked into the wasteland. I didn't touch her. She led me around a corner, where a breezeblock wall stood, and leant up against it. She almost fell against it. She pulled up her skirt in a bored manner, but by that time, I was trembling with excitement, and the knife was in my hand.

She didn't make a sound other than a small grunt as the blade sank in. It was me who made the noise: a groan muffled against the skin of her neck as the world swam away from me.

Chapter Nine

SOMETHING WAS WRONG. KATE CLOSED her eyes for a moment and then opened them again. She would normally open her eyes and find herself regarding her bedroom door. But, this morning, the spare bedside table was the first sight that met her eyes. Kate blinked. She had a few seconds of blissful ignorance, and then memory rushed back in to fill the gap. At the same moment, she became aware of Anderton's warm leg lying against hers beneath the covers. Kate shut her eyes tightly, cringing. *Oh God*. She'd ended up in bed with her boss. *Oh,* God.

She badly needed to pee, but she didn't want to wake him up. What the hell was she going to do?

After a few moments, she stealthily got up and crept from the room, bending double as if to hide her nakedness from the world.

In the bathroom, she took care of the pressing need of her bladder before checking her reflection. Tousled hair, flushed cheeks, the remnants of last night's make-up smeared under her eyes. Quickly, she swiped a flannel over her face and swished some mouthwash through her teeth.

"Morning," said the buried shape of Anderton as she got back into bed, wrapped in her dressing gown.

"Morning," said Kate, trying for casualness.

There was movement under the duvet, and then he turned to face her, smiling. Kate had a moment of disconnect: the surreal reality that was Anderton in her bed.

"What have you got that on for?" he asked, tugging at the dressing gown cord.

Kate mumbled something, a feeble protest that was rapidly lost as Anderton worked the cord loose and slid his hand underneath, pulling Kate towards him.

They were rapidly reaching a crucial point in the proceedings when a phone began to ring. For a few moments, they carried on until it became clear that the phone was going to keep ringing until someone answered it. Anderton cursed, rolled off Kate and snatched it up.

"Anderton," said Anderton, the gasp not quite gone from his voice. There a moment when the voice on the other end spoke, and Kate saw his shoulders stiffen. She sat up in bed slowly, pulling the covers up and tucking them under her arms, suddenly self-conscious. Anderton still hadn't spoken.

"Where?" he asked eventually. Then nothing until the voice paused, and he said "I'll be right down. Just get everyone that you can down there and try and hold off the press."

He pressed a button to terminate the call and placed his phone very slowly and precisely back on Kate's bedside table, still facing away from her.

"What is it?" said Kate, already knowing and yet still dreading the answer.

Anderton didn't turn around for a moment. Then he rolled back on the pillow and looked at her, his face very serious.

"It's another girl, isn't it," said Kate. A statement, not a question.

Anderton nodded. He put out an arm as if he were about to draw her down next to him and then something stopped the movement. Kate hadn't taken her eyes from his face.

"Is it the same—"

Anderton nodded.

"Same weapon. At least it looks that way. Same type, small and dark-haired."

"Oh, God." Kate wanted to get up but she felt shy about revealing her nakedness, absurdly. The whole tempo of their connection had suddenly changed – from passionate and romantic to grimly purposeful.

It felt wrong to be in bed with him, suddenly, as it hadn't done a moment before the phone call.

"Where was the body—"

Kate didn't seem to be able to finish a full sentence. Anderton understood her anyway.

"The same place. The warehouses, the rough ground."

Kate's eyes widened.

"But that's—"

"He's taking the *piss*!" said Anderton, cutting across her. He rolled violently out of bed and began to yank on his scattered clothes.

Kate watched, wanting to say something but not sure what, biting her lip. After he was dressed, Anderton looked as if he was about to head out of the bedroom door without even a goodbye. At the doorway, he stopped and then swung around and came back to the bed. He tipped Kate's chin up and kissed her, rather bruisingly.

"I need you there, Kate. Will you come?"

"Ye-yes," stuttered Kate, shaken a little by the violence of his kiss. Then she got a hold of herself.

"I'll come with you, shall I?"

Anderton shook his head.

"No, just get there when you can. Best we don't arrive together, eh?"

He gave her a rueful smile.

"Of course," said Kate bravely, to hide the quake

in the pit of her stomach. Was he saying he regretted what had happened?

"Good. See you soon."

He was out the bedroom door without another word. Kate waited until she heard the slam of the front door. Then she pushed back the covers and slowly swung her legs over the edge of the bed.

Under the streaming waters of the shower, she hung her head forward, letting the water roll over her face and closed eyes. There were too many emotions swirling around her head for Kate to even feel vaguely in control of herself. She made an effort, straightening up and trying to untangle how she felt.

Guilt. That was the main one. Guilt for having what could well turn out to be a one-night stand. She didn't *do* that sort of thing. No matter that she didn't *want* it to be a one-night stand. Sleeping with her boss – that was about the biggest no-no of them all. Okay, so she knew he was separated from his wife, but was he actually divorced? What about his children? Did he want a relationship with her, Kate, or was it going to be one of those dreadfully awkward working relationships where the fact that you'd once shagged meant you spent the rest of your career avoiding the subject with one another?

There was another, sharper layer of guilt too. Guilt that she'd been so distracted and so full of her own selfish inclinations that she'd not paid the attention to the case as she should have. And now another woman was dead. If Kate had been better at her job, worked harder, paid more attention – did that mean that they could have caught the man who was responsible already, caught him before he could kill again?

A small, reprehensible part of her wanted to relive the events of last night in detail, go over and over what had happened with a shiver of delight. And the juxtaposition of that feeling with the scene she now had to attend to was somehow the worst of all. What should have been a luxurious, sensual memory was now tainted.

For fuck's sake, Kate. Grow up and get a hold of yourself. You've got a job to do.

Kate dressed, pulling on sober clothes and brushing her hair back into its customary ponytail. The ache in unfamiliar places, the slight soreness when she moved was a constant reminder of what had happened last night.

There were other niggles as well, little jolts of uneasiness as memories surfaced. Kate hadn't had any condoms in the house – of course she hadn't, she hadn't had sex since 1995, or so it felt like – but Anderton had pulled a fresh packet from his jacket pocket. Why was he carrying them around? Of course, Kate knew there was only one reason that men carried condoms around. They were going to use them. And yes, she knew that it was the responsible thing to do but...but... He clearly wasn't celibate. Who was he seeing? One woman or many? Was he still sleeping with his wife? Oh *God*... Kate realised she was standing in the kitchen staring blankly at the hook on which her car keys hung. She shook herself back to reality and unhooked the keys.

As she started the car, her thoughts returned obsessively to Anderton's condom packet. Had he bought them at the pub before he walked her home? Did he plan to seduce her? Well, if he had, she'd made it pretty bloody easy for him, hadn't she? Where did she stand now, with him?

And why the bloody hell are you even worrying about this when you're about to visit a murder *scene?* She asked herself the question fiercely, gunning the accelerator.

It was a grey, nothing-y sort of morning, warm, humid and still. Kate parked the car a street away from the warehouses, wishing she'd eaten something or drunk a cup of coffee. She found a boiled sweet in her bag – where the hell had that come from? – and crunched it up. Blah, disgusting. What was wrong with her? Casual sex, drinking (albeit a fairly pathetic three glasses of champagne and half a glass of wine) and not bothering to eat breakfast? At least she was washed and dressed appropriately.

Kate dropped her head back against the back of the car seat for a moment. It was eight thirty eight in the morning and she was already exhausted. Then again, she hadn't exactly gotten much sleep last night. The thought provoked a guilty, half-gleeful smile, and she had to remind herself, yet again, that she was about to view a murder scene.

She was walking towards the waste ground when she realised she would be seeing Jerry for the first time since drenching him with wine. Her steps faltered before she remembered that he'd gone to Brighton for the day to check up on that similar case. Well, that was one thing to be thankful for. She could see the white plastic tent in the distance, the crime-scene tape girdling the scene, the various uniforms and plainclothes officers standing about. The flap of the tent was flung back and Anderton emerged, grim-faced. Kate's stomach flipped. She mentally shook herself. *There cannot be the slightest hint of what went on last night.* She took a deep breath and joined Olbeck and Jane and Rav where they were standing by the entrance to the tent.

"Morning."

Olbeck looked surprised to see her. He was opening his mouth to say something when Anderton shouted over.

"Kate! Over here, please."

"Talk to you in a sec," said Kate in an aside to Olbeck, not displeased at having to put off the inevitable questions. She walked over to where

Anderton stood by the tent's entrance, trying to keep a blank face, trying not to smile inappropriately.

Anderton wasn't smiling. He nodded towards what lay inside the tent, and Kate, saying nothing, ducked inside.

The tent was close and hot already. Kate looked at the body on the floor, and any thought of smiling left her. She felt the shock of it as if she'd swallowed a pint of ice-water.

The dead woman was Claudia Smith.

Chapter Ten

KATE DUCKED BACK OUT INTO the open air. Despite the warmth of the day, her face felt cold and stiff.

"It's Claudia Smith," she said to Anderton, as if he wouldn't already know.

He nodded and indicated for her to walk ahead of him, towards the others.

They stood in a group, looking at one another. Kate could see her emotions reflected in the others' faces: anger, guilt, bewilderment.

"Well," said Anderton. "This takes things to a new level, as I'm sure you can imagine."

"Who found her?" asked Olbeck.

"A dog walker. He was walking along the tow path, and his dog hared off here and went straight to the body, wouldn't come when called, so his owner followed him. We've taken him down to the station already to take his statement."

Kate stood clutching her elbows, her eyes cast down. A memory recurred: Claudia's look of pride as she watched her daughter clambering about on the climbing frame. Kate winced. She would not think about Madison and how she was now, essentially, an orphan.

"Kate?"

Kate looked up. Anderton was looking at her, and there was something tender in his gaze that both warmed and, conversely, alarmed her.

"I'm all right," she said.

"That's two girls who lived at the Mission," said Rav. "That can't be a coincidence. Can it?"

"Unlikely," said Anderton. "Now, let SOCO and the docs do their work here. Here's what we're going to do. Olbeck, Kate, you come with me to the Mission. Jane, go back to the office and dig up everything you can on our victim. Take Rav with you. Rav, pull all the CCTV footage from a mile-wide radius around this place. Go through it with a fine tooth comb. There must be *something* from last night."

Kate sat in the back of the car as usual, with Anderton driving and Olbeck riding shotgun. She looked at the back of the two men's heads, Olbeck's hair just a little too long, curling at the back of his neck, Anderton's grey mane neatly brushed. She remembered pushing her hands through his hair last night, bringing his face to hers. Kate jerked her gaze away, feeling her face heat up. She wondered what Anderton was thinking. Were his thoughts on the case or was he thinking about her? He met her gaze in the rear view mirror, and she snatched her glance away, knowing she was blushing and hating herself for it.

Margaret Paling met them at the door of the Mission, as if she'd been waiting for them to arrive. She was pale and wringing her hands.

"I'm so glad you're here," she said in a fervent whisper. "One of our girls is missing. She didn't turn up for work this morning and her bed's not been slept in—"

"Claudia Smith," said Anderton, sweeping past her.

"Yes, that's right," said Margaret, hurrying after him. "Has someone already told you? Oh. Oh no—"

She stopped, hands to her face. The police officers were already at the door of Father Michael's office. Through the glass door they could see that he was sat at his desk, staring unseeingly into space, his hands gripping the edge of the desk as if it were the only thing keeping him from falling.

He jumped up as the officers entered the room.

"You've found her? Please tell me you've found her?"

Anderton began to tell him of their grim discovery of the morning, speaking gently but inexorably. As he listened, Father Michael's eyes filled with tears. He turned, stumbled, put his hands out to break his fall and ended up on his knees, grasping his office chair.

"No, no, it can't – it can't be true—"

Kate and Olbeck exchanged glances. Anderton let them raise the man up to his feet and gently turn him around to face them. Father Michael was blinded by tears, the face of a drowning man coming up for his last gasp of air. He groped for his desk, sat down and buried his head in his arms.

After a few moments, Anderton asked, quietly, if Father Michael would be prepared to identify the body. He had to repeat the question.

"What?"

"Would you be prepared to identify the body, sir? You knew Claudia well."

Father Michael burst into fresh tears. He managed to nod over the flood.

"I'll do it. I have to – I have to see for myself."

He continued to cry, more quietly now, in the back of the car sat next to Kate. She was surprised at the level of impatience she felt for him. He was acting more like a bereaved father than someone who ran the hostel that accommodated the victim. She met Anderton's eyes in the mirror again but this time, there was no embarrassment. It was a mutual expression of *'what is going on here?'*

Although it was unusual for Kate, she decided to duck out of the actual identification. She wasn't sure she was up to seeing the fresh theatrics that the sight of Claudia's body would produce in Father

Michael. Sitting at her desk, she pulled herself up on that thought. Why *theatrics*? Why did that word come to mind?

Slowly she became aware that someone was speaking her name. With a jerk, she came back to reality to find Anderton at her shoulder.

"My office?"

Kate nodded, aware of Olbeck sitting down opposite her. He looked surprised to see her summoned by the boss. *If he only knew*, Kate thought as she followed Anderton to his office. Would he shut the door? For a moment, after she sat down, she thought he wouldn't, but he obviously changed his mind and shut it firmly.

There was a moment of tortuous silence.

"Kate—"

"Can I talk to you about Father Michael?" asked Kate, quickly.

Anderton blinked, sat back.

"Of course," he said, after a moment.

"What did you think?"

"Of his reaction?" Anderton watched her face, keeping her gaze. "I know what you mean."

"Do you think he could be bluffing?"

"It's possible."

"Don't you think it was over the top for someone who's supposed to have a fairly limited relationship with the victim?"

"Yes. It's not – not in character."

"Well, then..."

Silence fell. Kate tried desperately to think of something else to say. She could see Anderton gearing up to speak.

"Well, if that's everything," she said brightly, jumping up and making for the door.

"Wait. *Wait*."

Kate paused, her back to Anderton, her hand on the door handle. She was very aware of him walking up behind her, standing close enough for his breath to stir the hair on the back of her neck. Her hand slipped a little on the metal door handle.

"Aren't we even going to talk about it?" asked Anderton, speaking so softly she could barely hear him.

"Of course," muttered Kate. "It's just that—"

He leant forward and kissed the back of her neck, where the skin was exposed and her hair swept up into a ponytail. She lost the power of speech entirely.

"Turn around."

She couldn't move, could only shake her head mutely. He gently turned her round and kissed her, pressing her back against the door. Kate, while glorying in the sensation, was very aware that only three inches of wood and metal kept her colleagues and superiors from discovering what was going on. As soon as the thought flashed across Kate's brain, there was a knock at the door and Kate and

Anderton leapt apart as if propelled by an electric shock.

Kate, barely knowing what she was doing, went to sit back down at the desk. Anderton ran his hands through his hair and took a deep breath.

Rav barrelled in a moment later, waving a sheaf of papers.

"Sir," he said urgently, taking the spare chair by Kate. "CCTV from the night of the murder. You have to see this."

"What have we got?"

Anderton flung himself down in his chair and reached for the papers. Kate could almost admire the way he was acting, as if he and Kate had merely been talking about the case moments before, rather than pressed up against one another, panting and groping. It was very convincing. She then had the very unwelcome thought, *Perhaps he's done this before*.

She made an effort to concentrate on what Rav was saying.

"Look here. And here. The same car."

Anderton studied the print-outs alertly.

"This is last night?"

Rav shook his head.

"No. I've not been able to get that yet. But this is the night that Mandy Renkin was killed. This car was seen very close to the warehouses and look here—" He pointed to a blurry image of a dark-haired girl sat in the passenger seat of the car in question. "Doesn't that look very like her?"

Anderton brought the picture closer to his face.

"It does," he said quietly. "Now tell me you know who this car is registered to, Rav."

Rav was grinning.

"Of course. Address of the owner is Twenty six Lavender Street, Charlock."

Kate gasped. Anderton's fist curled, crumpling the paper.

"I *knew* it," he growled. "Father Michael. Is he still here?"

"No, Jane dropped him back at the Mission."

"Well, get him back here. Right now."

Rav was already heading towards the door. Kate got up, chewing her thumbnail. Her head was in a whirl: Anderton's kisses, Father Michael's car and the small, curled body of Claudia Smith all vied for her attention. She felt dizzy.

She was at the door when Anderton spoke her name, but this time she looked back, smiled and shook her head before she left the room.

Chapter Eleven

FATHER MICHAEL TOOK THE CHAIR falteringly. He looked around at the breezeblock walls painted an indifferent cream, the scuffed linoleum on the floor, the screwed down table with the air of man in a waking nightmare. He kept blinking, as if the harsh light from the strip light overhead hurt his eyes.

Anderton and Kate sat down opposite him and the duty solicitor.

Anderton began.

"Father Michael Brannigan, are you aware of why we've brought you in for questioning today?"

Father Michael was still looking about him. He folded his trembling hands in front of him on the table.

"Yes. Yes, you want to talk to me about Claudia." He looked directly at them both, his resonant voice suddenly gaining in strength and assurance. "I assure you that I did not kill her."

Anderton ignored his statement.

"How long have you known Claudia Smith?"

Father Michael blinked again.

"She's been at the Mission for a while. Perhaps six months? I would have to check the records."

"Did you know her before she came to live at the Mission?"

"Yes. Yes, well, very slightly. She used to attend a mother and baby group that the church ran at a local village hall, and I believe I first met her then, when she came along with her daughter."

Anderton nodded. His manner changed slightly, became more conspiratorial, more...matey.

"So you have known her some time, Father? Would you say you were friends?"

Father Michael smiled, rather tremulously.

"Friends? Well, I'm not sure that would be the right term. The disparity in our ages and circumstances... I liked her. I felt sorry for her and Madison. There was so much stacked against them."

"How so?"

Father Michael's smile vanished.

"She had a tragic past, you know. Not much family support, no real role model at home. She got into a relationship with a man who treated her appallingly."

"That was Madison's father?"

Father Michael nodded.

"Have you questioned *him*? He was a monster,

violent, abusive. Has *he* been questioned about her death?"

"Enquiries are continuing," said Anderton smoothly, the usual response to that sort of question. He leant forward a little. "So you wouldn't say you were close friends with Claudia?"

"No – not as such, no."

Anderton sat back.

"What about Mandy Renkin?"

Kate was watching Father Michael's face closely. He didn't look shocked or guilty, merely blank.

"Mandy?"

"Would you say you were close friends?"

"No. Not at all. She was a young woman who lived at the Mission, that's all. I wished her well, I was concerned with her welfare but not – nothing much more."

Anderton brought his hand out from under the table. He was holding the print outs from the CCTV of Father Michael's car taken on the night of Mandy Renkin's death. He threw them onto the table in front of the priest and the slippery paper slid into a fan shape of dark images on the table top.

"So what was she doing in your car on the night of her death, Father?" he asked quietly.

Father Michael looked at the papers, seemingly uncomprehendingly.

"I – I don't—" he began.

"This is your car. Seen in the area of the crime,

on the night of Mandy's death, with Mandy Renkin in the front seat."

"I—"

"What explanation do you have for this?"

Father Michael was silent for a long moment.

"I – it—"

Whatever excuse he had tried to come up with was discarded. Kate could see it in his face: the realisation that whatever reason he brought up just wouldn't wash.

"Is this your car?" continued Anderton, relentless.

After a moment, Father Michael nodded wordlessly.

"Speak up, please."

"I'm sorry, yes. Yes, it's my car."

"Can you explain what it was doing in the vicinity of the crime scene on the night Mandy Renkin died? Is that Mandy in the front seat?"

Again, that moment of wordlessness. Kate could see the man sat opposite her thinking hard. Was he working out his excuse or thinking up a plausible lie?

"That is my car," said Father Michael eventually. "But that's not Mandy."

Anderton narrowed his eyes. "It's not? Who is it then?"

"It's Claudia."

"Claudia Smith?" A nod from Father Michael.

He clasped and unclasped his hands, suddenly an old man. "What was she doing in your car?"

Father Michael cleared his throat.

"I was just giving her a lift."

"Where?"

"To – to a friend's house."

"Who is this friend?"

"She didn't say. She just – just asked if I could give her a lift. It was a cold night, I didn't want her to walk, so – so I said I would."

"Where did you drop her off?"

Father Michael was staring at the CCTV printouts as if they fascinated him.

"I'm sorry?"

"Where did you drop Claudia off?" repeated Anderton.

"I – I don't remember."

"Whereabouts?"

"I'm sorry. I can't remember."

He was lying. Kate pressed the side of her foot against Anderton's shoe, the usual way she had of communicating with him. A second later, she realised, as she never had before, that she was essentially playing footsie with him and snatched her boot away as if his shoe had been red hot. It had done the trick though; he turned very slightly to her and she communicated her scepticism to him in a direct, wordless look. He nodded very slightly.

"I want to talk to my solicitor," said Father

Michael, slightly too loudly. "Alone. That's allowed, isn't it?"

Left alone, Kate suddenly felt the awkwardness between Anderton and herself. Or she told herself she felt it. Did she really know what he was thinking? Would she ever?

Impulsively she turned to him and opened her mouth, but before she could say anything, he gave her a miniscule shake of the head, indicating with his finger the camera in the corner of the room. Chastened, Kate sat back in her chair.

Father Michael and his solicitor had only been away for five minutes, but in the silence that swamped the interview room during their departure, it felt more like five years to Kate. She'd never before been so pleased to see a suspect reappear.

Father Michael sat back down again in the same chair he'd had before. He folded his hands in front of him again, but they were steadier than they had been before.

"I've something to tell you," he announced with a glance at his solicitor, who gave him a slight nod.

"Yes?" Anderton sat up a little.

Father Michael cleared his throat.

"Claudia and I – Claudia and I were – we were in a relationship. Having a relationship."

He pressed his lips together as if he were unwilling to say more.

Anderton raised his eyebrows.

"Care to elaborate?"

The tone of Anderton's voice must have stung. Kate watched the blood rise in Father Michael's cheeks, visible even behind his beard.

"I – well, we – we were in a relationship, like I said."

"A sexual relationship?"

"Yes." Father Michael's face was fiery now, and for the first time, Kate felt a twinge of pity for him.

"How long had this been going on?"

Father Michael cleared his throat again.

"Not very long. Several months, I suppose. Perhaps six months."

"You can't remember exactly?"

"Well, I – no, not exactly." Father Michael pulled his folded hands under the table, away from their eyes. Kate knew it was because his hands were trembling again.

He went on, falteringly.

"We go – we used to go to a hotel near Arbuthon Green. That was where we were driving on the night of Mandy's death. That was why we were in the area and why Claudia was in my car."

Anderton kept his eyes on the man's hot face.

"What was the name of the hotel?"

"It was nowhere very expensive, nothing – nothing showy."

"That's not what I asked."

"Yes. Sorry. It's called The Pines.'"

"You stayed there how often?"

Father Michael's flush had been fading, but now it returned in a renewed, rosy hue.

"A few times a week. Sometimes on weekends. It depended on whether she could get anyone to look after her daughter."

"Anyone?"

"Well, her mother. She would only let her mother look after Madison. She was very protective of her."

His voice shook, and he looked down at his hidden hands. Despite herself, Kate was wrenched momentarily with pity. She tried not to think of Madison and her solemn little face, her big dark eyes. What would they have told her? How do you break something like that to a little child?

Anderton began the questioning again but Kate, drifting off a little, found herself picturing Father Michael and Claudia. Actually picturing them in bed together. Thirty years or more between them: education, class, even intelligence perhaps a chasm between them. Why had he pursued her? Or had it been the other way around? Had he been kind to her, poor Claudia, who had been so dreadfully treated by another man? Now Kate remembered going to interview her about Mandy Renkin, the way that Claudia had flung her bedroom door open in happy anticipation. She must have thought it was Father Michael who'd knocked.

What a risk he had taken, though, this priest who was supposed to be celibate, above the temptations of the flesh. No such thing, as Kate had good reason to know.

Her colleagues would be crawling all over the Mission now, checking computers and laptops and offices, digging into everything to try and prove a connection with the killings. Kate turned her attention back to Anderton, who was wrapping up this session of questioning.

"I think we'll take a break, there," he said, shuffling his papers into a rough stack. Father Michael sat back in his chair, raising his hands to his eyes. His solicitor bent forward and picked up her briefcase.

Kate was the first out in the corridor. She stood aside as Father Michael was escorted back to the cells; they would hold him for another twenty-four hours and then either charge him with the murders of Claudia Smith and Mandy Renkin or release him. She watched his thin figure disappear as the heavy door to the cells closed behind him. Was it possible that this stooped, bearded man was actually a serial killer?

"Got a minute?" asked Anderton, directly behind her, and Kate jumped.

They went to Anderton's office, but this time, he didn't close the door. Obviously there were to be no illicit kisses this time. Kate sat down at his desk, feeling a slow droop of her spirits.

Anderton flung himself into the opposite chair and began to flick through the paperwork.

"Can you get over to Brannigan's house tomorrow and start going through it?" he asked, his eyes scanning the papers before him. "Take Theo – oh wait, of course you can't. Take Rav and Jane and make a start."

Kate waited to see if he'd say anything else, something personal, something intimate. He didn't. He didn't even look at her.

"Yes, sir," she said, numbly, and got up to go. Unable to help herself, she looked back as she reached the doorway. Anderton still had his head down, intent on his work. Kate hesitated and then left, swallowing hard against the thickening in her throat.

Chapter Twelve

THE GOOD WEATHER TURNED THE next day; June's blue skies were obscured with thick grey clouds and spitting rain. Kate dug her summer raincoat out from beneath the pile of jackets and scarves that hung on the back of the downstairs toilet door and put it on. She sat on the bottom step of the staircase to lace up her trainers, caught sight of the time on her wristwatch and cursed. She was supposed to be picking Rav up at nine and he lived a good twenty minutes' drive from her place. It was already eight forty-five.

She sent him a quick text telling him she was running late, grabbed her car keys and locked up the house. She knew why she was late, which was most unlike her. She'd spent the night rolling from one side of the bed to another, trying to get comfortable, trying to ignore the gnawing in the pit of her stomach.

This is what happens when you get involved, *Kate,* she told herself. Months, no, *years* of happy equilibrium and celibacy and then one night of passion and it all goes to pot...

As was usual when one was in a hurry, the traffic was heavy, and every traffic light disobligingly went red as Kate approached it. She tapped her fingers on the steering wheel, gritting her teeth. Eventually, she drew into the driveway of the block of flats, drove into a parking space and beeped the horn. Kate raised her hand as Rav's flatmate, whom she knew very slightly, passed the car, obviously on his way to work. Then Rav knocked on her window, making her jump.

"Morning!"

"Hi," said Kate, smiling in spite of herself. Rav was the youngest member of the team, barely into his twenties. He'd joined the police force straight after sixth form college and barely looked any older than he had when he'd left school. Kate didn't have much in common with him, but they worked together well. She liked his energy and enthusiasm.

Whilst Rav strapped himself in, Kate tapped the postcode to Father Michael's house into the sat nav.

"Jane's meeting us there," she said. "Mind if we stop on the way and grab a coffee?"

"Nope, no problem." Rav looked slyly across at her and grinned. "As long as you don't throw it in my face."

Kate thought she'd misheard him for a moment.

She looked over, eyebrows raised – and then she got it.

"Oh, ha bloody ha. Oh, my aching sides."

She snorted and put her foot down harder on the accelerator.

"What *happened* with you and Jerry?" asked Rav, clearly burning with curiosity, which Kate was not about to satisfy. She waved a hand in a dismissive manner.

"Not much," she said. "Storm in a tea-cup. Or a wine glass."

Rav giggled. "It was just so totally not like you. We couldn't believe it."

"Oh well," said Kate, uncomfortably. "Did you guys stay on much longer?"

"Yeah, 'til closing time. And *then* we went clubbing."

"Jerry went clubbing?"

"Yeah, I know, not like him, is it?" Rav pushed a hand through his thick, black hair. "Seriously, it was daylight by the time we all rolled out of the club. I'm still hungover now."

"Mmm-hmm," said Kate, having heard enough about Jerry. She wanted to forget that part of the night altogether if she could.

Rav checked his phone.

"We're still holding this priest, yeah?"

"That's right," said Kate. "Anderton wants us to go through his house with a fine-tooth comb."

They drove in silence for a minute. Then Rav spoke up.

"This is pretty bad, isn't it, Kate? This case, I mean."

Kate glanced over.

"Yes, it's bad. It's the worst I've dealt with since I started here."

Rav was looking out the window at the streets of Abbeyford as they rolled by.

"We don't get cases like this here," he said. "I mean, do we? Serial killings...that's something that happens to other towns, not here."

"Well," said Kate. "I suppose it doesn't happen here...until it happens here."

"What if—" said Rav, and then he hesitated. Kate looked at him enquiringly.

"What?"

"What if it's not a serial killing?"

Kate was drawing onto the street on which Michael Brannigan lived. She parked the car, switched off the engine and turned to face Rav more fully.

"What do you mean?"

"Well, it's only an idea," said Rav nervously. "And I'm not saying the murders aren't related, I mean, they are – they clearly are. But what if the girls died for some other reason? Something we haven't found yet."

Kate thought it through. It was an intriguing

idea, and she said as much to Rav, earning a pleased smile.

"Maybe we'll have a clearer picture once we've done the search," she said. "But it's certainly an idea. We should bear it in mind."

"Will you tell the boss?"

"Me?" said Kate sharply. "Why would I need to tell him? Why me?"

Rav looked surprised at her tone, as well he might.

"Oh, no reason," he said, climbing out of the car. "I just thought you might mention it. It might sound better coming from you."

That remark followed Kate into the house. Why had Rav said that? Kate snapped on her gloves on auto-pilot. The forensic team would have already been over the house, taking their samples and fingerprints and photographs. Looking closely, Kate could see the faint dusting of fingerprint powder, the odd smear and scuff on the walls and windows. The room had that slightly ruffled look of a place that had been thoroughly searched by experts.

Kate moved carefully through the hallway and into the front room. Rav stayed by the front door, running his practised eyes over the hallway furniture, the pile of worn shoes and scuffed boots by the coat stand. Kate stood for a moment in the centre of the living room, trying to concentrate. *It might sound better coming from you*. What did Rav mean? Surely nobody could know. Could they? She felt suddenly feverish with anxiety. Surely Anderton wouldn't have told anyone? Would he?

Concentrate, Kate. She went to the bookcase, always a good place to start. There was a real jumble of books on the shelves, an assortment of classics, non-fiction and an unsurprising number of religious works. She ran her finger along the spines and then began to work methodically through the books, taking them out and shaking them. It was repetitive work, and her mind soon began to wander. To Anderton, inevitably. She took out her phone in the ridiculous hope that he had sent her a message. Of course he hadn't, although there was a text from Olbeck, which said, *training tonight ok? Pick u up @ 7pm x*

For the first time, Kate found she was actually looking forward to going running later. She wanted to be out in the fresh air, moving from one foot to the other, eyes fixed on the horizon and not thinking about anything to do with her boss, or murdered girls, or how she seemed to have messed up her life yet again. She texted Olbeck back an affirmative with a kiss on the end and then turned her attention back to the search.

Jane had arrived by now, and she waved to Kate before heading upstairs to the bedrooms. Kate could hear her footsteps creaking the floorboards above her. This was an old house, Victorian in age, and chilly despite the time of year. The carpet was clean, but threadbare; the sofa was an old Ikea model with a checked Welsh blanket tucked over it. It was obviously the home of a man with limited spare cash – on the face of it, the home of a man who was cultured and intelligent and thrifty. Could it also be the home of a man who had murdered two – perhaps even three – women?

Kate's phone rang, and when she saw Anderton's name on the little screen, her heart gave a thump that was almost painful. She made herself wait for three rings before she answered it.

"Sir?"

"Anything?"

"Sorry?"

"Found anything?"

Kate clenched her teeth for a moment. So this was how he was going to play it, was he? Pretend the whole thing never happened. Was it because she'd walked out of his office when he wanted to talk to her? Was he really that petty?

"Not yet, *sir*," she said.

"Okay, that's fine. I need you to get over to the PM – Mark and I are tied up here with questioning. Can you do that?"

"Of course," Kate said coldly.

"Good. See you later."

The line went dead.

Kate put the phone back in her pocket. Her

throat was aching and for a moment she stared at the opposite wall through a mist of tears that she blinked rapidly away. Just as well, as Rav came through from the kitchen moments later.

In the car on her way to to the pathology lab, Kate found herself grinding her teeth in rage, both at herself and at Anderton. *You idiot, Kate. You know what happened in Bournemouth, you swore it wouldn't happen again, and yet here you are, making the same stupid mistakes. Don't you ever* learn? She repeated the last sentence out loud and then she yelled it. Unfortunately the car was stationary at the time, and she caught the gaze of an astonished elderly gentlemen, who was crossing the road in front of her and clearly perplexed at the sight of a red-faced women shouting at herself in the rear view mirror. Kate forced a smile as he shuffled away, staring back over his shoulder until mercifully the lights changed and she was able to accelerate out of his sightline.

Unwelcome memories assailed her as she drew into the car park of her destination. For the first time in a few days, she remembered Jerry's sneer and his accusatory words. *"Why would I like, much less respect someone who gets ahead by getting on her back?" There's no truth to that,* Kate told herself stoutly as she locked the car door. *No truth at all.* But, thinking back, she had to admit that it was possible Jerry might have got hold of the wrong end of the stick. There had been enough innuendo and rumour flying around for a while, after all. And hadn't he once been based in Brighton? It wasn't beyond the realms of possibility that he'd heard what had happened.

Nothing much *had* happened. Kate, like so many people, had had a short affair with one of her colleagues in Bournemouth. A ridiculous, disastrous affair that lasted all of six weeks. And yes, she admitted to herself as she went into the reception area of the labs, she'd fallen into bed with someone who was technically her superior. And yes, she admitted to herself as she flashed her warrant card and was directed up to one of the theatres on the first floor, she'd obtained her transfer and promotion quite soon after that affair had ended. But, and she was absolutely clear on this, her promotion had been gained entirely on her own merit. The way the affair had ended, she'd been lucky to get any kind of reference at all.

When she considered explaining this to Jerry, however, she was forced to give herself a mental slap in the face. *You made a mistake then, you made one now. Learn from it and move on, Kate. When you next see Anderton, be professional, be courteous and be distant.* She arrived outside the door she was seeking and smoothed back her hair.

The pathologist conducting the autopsy of

Claudia Smith was Andrew Stanton, and if Kate hadn't been in such a neurotic and anxious state, the pleased expression when he saw who had come to act as a police presence might have both amused and irritated her. As it was, she barely noticed, automatically returning his greeting. Her gaze was drawn, inevitably, to the small body of Claudia Smith, which lay supine on the hard metal surface of the table.

For the first time in an hour, all thoughts of Kate's romantic troubles fled. She was struck, as she so often was at post mortems, by the intense vulnerability of the corpse. Claudia looked so young; of course, she had *been* young, but her body looked tiny, diminished in death. She had given birth to a child, but her shallow-breasted, narrow-hipped body looked too young and undeveloped to have done so. Stripped of that awful makeup, the fake tan washed away, her body had achieved a kind of morbid beauty; the purity of her profile suggested the blanched, sculpted face of a marble statue.

Andrew Stanton had a brusque, no-nonsense method of working; his hands were less gentle than the delicate fingers of Doctor Telling. Kate waited and watched, listening to the doctor commenting on his findings, trying not to wince. Occasionally she asked a question.

"When was she killed?"

Doctor Stanton was rinsing a scalpel and

the knife clattered against the tap with a ringing metallic sound.

"Between 2:00 a.m. and 3:30 a.m., the night before last. I can't narrow it down much further than that, I'm afraid."

"That's fine," said Kate. "So she was killed in the hours of darkness? It starts to get light about four thirty at the moment, doesn't it?"

"Yep," said Stanton. "Summer solstice has just passed, I think."

Kate nodded.

"Any sign of sexual assault?"

"Not that I could find. She'd had a child, as I expect you know."

Kate nodded, thrusting the thought of Madison's lost little face away with an effort. Stanton, having finished the autopsy, pulled the green sheet up over the body, hiding Claudia's face away.

Kate rubbed her finger over her top lip, thinking.

"No sign of sexual assault at all?" she asked.

Stanton looked at her with surprise.

"No. Didn't I just say?"

"Yes. Yes, you did, sorry. I was just thinking..." She trailed off. No sign of sexual assault on Mandy's body either, although hadn't Doctor Telling found traces of lubricant? What did that mean? Had the killer raped or had sex with Mandy? Why not with Claudia? Was that significant?

It's probably nothing, thought Kate. Mandy was

a prostitute. She'd probably had sex with another punter before she met the one who killed her.

She came to with a start, realising Doctor Stanton was speaking to her.

"So that's all sorted, right?"

"Sorry?" asked Kate.

"My report. I'll have it to you in the next couple of days, okay?"

"Right. Great," said Kate, still thinking.

Andrew Stanton took off his lab coat and threw it into the laundry basket by the sink. He switched from his professional manner to his usual semi-jokey, flirtatious banter.

"So," he said, "It's dinner on Friday, right?"

He always said that, and Kate normally treated it like a little joke they shared, refusing him in the same joshing manner. She opened her mouth to give her usual, humorous refusal. She suddenly thought of her last, clipped conversation with Anderton, felt a rush of misery and found her mouth saying to the good doctor, "Why not? I'd like to."

The look on Andrew Stanton's face made Kate wish she'd agreed before. He goggled for a moment before rallying quite magnificently.

"Seriously? I mean, great. Great! Seriously?" He looked at Kate's face. "Well, that's great. When shall I pick you up?"

Back in her car and driving back towards her

house, Kate found herself giggling despite herself. Then she took herself in hand. *You shouldn't have done that, Kate. You don't feel like that about him, you're giving him false hope.* She slowed down for a junction, caught her own gaze in the mirror and found herself saying out loud, "Oh fuck *off.* I'm entitled to think of myself for once. It could be a nice evening."

She caught herself wondering how she could contrive to let Anderton know she'd got a date for Friday evening. Then the memory of poor Claudia on the autopsy table reoccurred, and she didn't think much about anything else for a time.

J's diary

IT'S FUNNY. THE FURTHER ALONG in my journey I get, the shorter the time I spend in my transformed state. By which I mean that glorious Technicolor feeling of really living after each time is getting shorter and shorter. Grey reality began to intrude mere days after I killed Claudia. It felt so unfair, as I'd had such a lovely time planning it. The anticipation was almost better than the actual event. Now it's over and done with, and the colour is draining back out of the world, the black clouds are gathering.

It would be wonderful if there could be some way of filming what I do so I could watch it over and over again. Of course, it wouldn't be the same as actually doing it, but it might tide me over for a few more weeks. I'm beginning to feel the urge again now, and there's no one suitable in sight. It makes me itchy and frustrated and I find myself pacing around the house in the evenings, drinking whisky and holding the knife in my hand. Plunging it into something soft, stabbing a pillow for example, brings a mere flicker of the real thing; it's not enough. And yet, how can I get the real thing when I haven't even found the next one yet?

It worries me because the worse the longing gets, the more likely it is that I'll succumb without having planned it all first. I simply cannot be caught. I *need* to go on doing this. It's the only thing that makes life worth living.

Chapter Thirteen

KATE WAS SO BUSY WORRYING about Claudia and Anderton and why they didn't seem to be getting anywhere with this case that she had completely forgotten that today was the day Jerry got back from Brighton. She walked quite confidently into the office, shoulders back, determined not to let Anderton know how she was feeling. Raising a hand to Rav at his desk, she swallowed hard when she saw Jerry sat opposite him. He looked up as if drawn by her gaze, gave her a blank stare for a moment and then turned his eyes back to his computer screen.

Kate fumbled her own chair out from under her desk and sat down shakily. Luckily, there were only a few people in the office to witness her discomfort. She sat it out for a few minutes, head bent down studiously, reading the same report over and over again without taking in a word of it, before deciding to head up to the viewing room. She wanted to see what was happening with the questioning of

Michael Brannigan. And she wanted a coffee. That was it. No other reason.

She forced herself to go up to Rav and Jerry and ask them if they wanted a drink. Jerry ignored her, and Rav shook his head with an embarrassed smile. Kate smiled back brightly and wheeled around, marching from the room.

Up in the viewing room, she collapsed in front of the screens with a sigh. The sight of Anderton, even on CCTV footage, made a tide of longing rise up within her. She brought her coffee cup up to her lips, scalding her throat as she gulped.

"The receptionist at the Pines Hotel has made a tentative identification of you and Claudia Smith," Anderton was saying.

Father Michael leaned forward.

"That's good. Yes, we stayed there several times."

Anderton nodded slightly.

"The only trouble is," he went on. "Is that she is unable to confirm your presence there on the night of Mandy Renkin's death."

Kate saw Father Michael's knuckles whiten as his clasped hands clenched.

"Well, we were there," he said after a moment. "We were there all night."

"So you say. But the problem is that we have no way of confirming that fact. Did you sign the guest book?"

Kate reluctantly smiled. She knew damn well

that the guest book would have been one of the first things he checked.

Brannigan shook his head.

"Well, why was that?" asked Anderton.

"I would have thought it was obvious."

"You didn't want anyone to know you were staying there. I see. The trouble is, Father, is that without a definite identification that night, with no record of your visit, we only have your word for it that you were ever there."

"Yes, I know—"

"When you were first asked your whereabouts on the night in question, you told our officers that you were at home alone, all night."

Father Michael's head dropped forward. He spoke so softly that Kate could barely hear his words.

"I lied."

"Yes," said Anderton, and he let the pause after his comment spool out for a few uncomfortable seconds. The implication was clear – that Father Michael was lying about everything.

Kate had seen enough. She dropped her empty coffee cup in the recycling bin and headed downstairs to her desk.

Rav had gone somewhere else when she got back to the office and only Jerry remained. Kate sighed inwardly. Then, mentally preparing herself, she walked up to Jerry.

"Hi."

He ignored her. Kate gritted her teeth.

"I'm sorry about the other night."

He still ignored her. *Fine, if that's the way you want to play it.*

"Can I borrow the file on Ingrid Davislova if you have it? Please?"

For a moment, Kate thought Jerry was going to continue to ignore her. Then, without raising his head or acknowledging her in any other way, he threw a cardboard folder across the desk at her.

"Thanks," muttered Kate. *You grumpy old fucker.* She took the file back to her desk and sat down.

Kate pulled the cardboard folder towards her and opened it. There was frighteningly little inside it. Just another case of a forgotten woman, someone who fell through the cracks, someone unimportant to those who have the power.

Was that what this killer was doing? Was he purposefully targeting the forgotten ones, the ones no one cared about? He wouldn't be the first. *There's a reason a lot of serial killers target prostitutes*, Kate remembered Anderton saying. *They're accessible and they're forgettable. And there's still a section of society who think that they deserve everything they get.* Kate remembered the serial killings in Ipswich in 2006, the headlines screaming, 'Prostitutes

Killed' and the articles that referred to the victims as 'murdered prostitutes,' as if the fact that those woman had sold sex was the only thing that would ever define them – not the fact that they were mothers, daughters, sisters, aunts and friends.

Kate resettled her face from the frown than had emerged while she thought. She leafed slowly through the paperwork in the folder, looking for something, anything that might give her a clue to this killer.

She'd been reading for almost an hour when she spotted it. In the pathologist's report, he'd mentioned a small bruise on the victim's upper chest, just under her collarbone. In the usual medical jargon, the doctor had pointed out the unusual shape of the bruising, quite clearly the shape of a butterfly or moth. He speculated that it had been caused by a metal button, or badge, or brooch that was shaped like the insect, and suspected that it had pressed hard enough into Ingrid Davislova's flesh that the blood vessels beneath her skin were broken into the shape of the pattern. Kate stared at the pictures from the PM, the close-up shots of the mark, blotchy purple against pallid skin. She traced the shape with her finger nail. Why there? She touched the site of the bruise on her own skin. Surely that button or brooch or whatever it was had been pinned or sewn to the killer's jacket lapel. Ingrid had been stabbed from the front, facing her murderer – just like the others. Kate checked the medical report again. Ingrid had been one hundred and sixty seven centimetres tall, or about five feet and six inches, so if the bruise was at lapel height on her, then the killer must be much the same height. Was that right? Kate considered, chewing her thumb nail.

She found the pathologist reports from the autopsies of Mandy Renkin and Claudia Smith. There was nothing in them regarding a butterfly-shaped bruise. Was she just chasing shadows, looking for something that didn't exist? Kate rubbed her eyes. So – what about *these* women? They were all young, all small and slight, all with long, dark hair. They were all killed in out-of-the-way places: waste grounds, back alleys, places where most people didn't go, or if they did, not at night. Was that significant? Did they meet their killer there, and if so, *why*? Did they know their killer? Kate tapped her pen on her teeth. They must have done, surely? Why would you meet someone in what was essentially a rather sinister and dangerous place if you didn't trust them?

Which brought her back to Father Michael. He'd known both Abbeyford victims; he was in a position of authority. He was someone that they would trust. Kate found it hard to imagine the tall, thin man plunging a knife into anyone, but people were very often not how they appeared. Everyone had something hidden inside them: good or bad. For a moment, Kate remembered Anderton poised above her, his expression one she had never seen before. The strength of his hands, gripping her wrists.

She allowed herself a moment's luxurious remembrance and then dismissed the thought, turning her attention back to the files in front of her. Something nagged at her, something she'd recently noticed. Flipping the pages of the report in front of her, she remembered. The button-shaped bruise on Ingrid Davislova. If Father Michael had worn that on his lapel, then how could it have bruised Ingrid's chest? He was a foot taller than she was. Perhaps he'd pinned it lower down. But why would he?

Kate leaned forward, head in her hands, eyes scanning the words she'd looked at before. She had the feeling, growing for a while now, that she'd let these women down. No, the whole *team* had let these women down. They'd failed to catch the killer after Mandy Renkin's death, and now he'd killed again. She dug deep, forcing an acknowledgement. Was it because these women weren't important to anyone that no one had worked their hardest? That no one had really had the passion to see the case through to a successful conclusion? Or was there some other reason, some other reason why nothing seemed to be working?

Kate blew out her cheeks and stood up, fed up with it all. Olbeck looked up from his desk.

"What's up?"

"Nothing. I'm just frustrated, that's all. Thought I'd spotted something significant and now, I don't know..."

"What is it?"

Kate brought the files over to Olbeck's desk and told him about the butterfly bruise.

"Did it show up on any of the others?"

Kate shook her head.

"Well, then," said Olbeck, reasonably. "How does it help us?"

"Oh, I don't bloody know," said Kate. She got up again. "I'm going out for a bit."

Olbeck pushed back his chair.

"I'll come with you. I could murder a coffee. Whoops, bad phrasing. I could do with a caffeinated beverage, I mean."

They walked down to the local greasy spoon and found a wobbly table out on the grimy stretch of pavement at the front of the shop. Kate took care of the seats while Olbeck got the drinks.

Kate stirred her cappuccino and told Olbeck what she'd just been thinking.

"Seriously?" he asked. "You think we've all been – well, slacking a bit?"

"I didn't exactly mean that," said Kate,

uncomfortably. "But it's just – why aren't we further forward in the case? It feels like whatever we do, something is – I don't know – *blocking* us from getting any further."

Olbeck was looking mystified.

"I'm not sure what you mean."

Kate shrugged. "I don't know exactly what I mean either. It's just a feeling, really."

"Feelings aren't evidence. If you're saying we should have caught him before he killed again then yes, of course I agree with you. But we're not superhuman, Kate. We can only go so far and so fast. You know that. We can't go hauling everyone who might even be vaguely guilty of something."

"Yes, I know." Kate drew a spiral in the foam of her coffee cup with the handle of a teaspoon. She gestured to it.

"That's us," she said. "Going round in ever decreasing circles."

"Listen," said Olbeck, leaning forward. "Maybe we are a bit out of our depth, I don't know. It's not like we get a lot of these cases in Abbeyford, thank God. Perhaps we ought to talk to Anderton. Perhaps we need more expert guidance."

Kate raised her eyebrows.

"Call in the Yard?"

"If necessary. It might happen anyway."

"Hmm."

Olbeck looked a little annoyed. "Well, what do

you suggest then? You think we're not getting very far. For what it's worth, I agree. What do you think we should do?"

Kate stirred the dregs of her coffee moodily. She was starting to regret saying anything.

"What can we do? Just more of the same but more thoroughly. Talk to the people who knew the victims. Check alibis, check CCTV. Find something that connects them."

"We know what connects them. Father Michael."

"He's guilty of having an affair with Claudia Smith. We can't prove he's guilty of her murder."

Olbeck sat back in his chair, blowing out his cheeks.

"Maybe we're looking at this the complete wrong way. We're assuming it's a serial killer. What if it's not?"

Kate looked at him narrowly. "What do you mean?"

"Is it possible that these deaths are actually coincidental?"

"Oh, come on," scoffed Kate. "Same MO, same weapon, same victim type?"

Olbeck stared into the middle distance for a moment. Then he grimaced and threw up his hands.

"You're right. It's a stupid idea."

"Well, if it's ideas you're looking for, then I'm clean out."

The two of them were silent, regarding the empty,

foam-caked cups before them. Kate, inevitably, felt her thoughts being drawn back to Anderton. For a mad moment, she opened her mouth to tell Olbeck, and then sanity returned and she shut it with a snap.

"Come on," said Olbeck. "Let's get back."

They walked the short distance back to the office in silence. Kate felt depressed, heavy with regrets and unspoken thoughts. She and Olbeck had never really had any secrets before. Now there was a big one between them. Now, there was distance.

J's diary

I CAN REMEMBER WHEN I FIRST found heard about John. I was seven years old – could I really have been only seven? – and it was an incredibly blustery rainy day, the water falling from the sky in rippling sheets. Mrs H, who'd popped round for her usual cup of tea and gossip session with Mother, had almost been blown in the front door, shrieking and dripping water all over the floor. I'd come to the doorway of the dining room and stood there, silently watching, until Mother and Mrs H had looked over and frowned to see me, their usual expression whenever they regarded me.

"Go to your room," Mother said sharply. I turned and trudged up the stairs as they went through into the kitchen. I heard Mother muttering something about my behaviour as they disappeared from view.

"...at the end of my tether, that child is so underhand. I sometimes think there's something really wrong with—"

Her voice faded out of my hearing, and I couldn't

hear Mrs H's reply. I paused at the top of the stairs, my fists clenched. For some reason I thought of Mrs H's son, who was younger than me, although only by a few years. For a while, we'd been allowed to play together, but that had stopped suddenly. I wasn't that fussed about it, to be honest. He was a bit of a cry-baby and never wanted to play the games that I did.

I turned and crept back down the stairs. I wasn't going to be sent to my room like a baby. I was only seven, but already I was creeping around, listening at doors and overhearing things that perhaps I wasn't meant to hear. Looking back, I know now that it was the only way I could retain some power, the only way I could have something of my own that Mother didn't know about.

I tiptoed up to the kitchen door, which was slightly ajar. Mrs H and Mother were talking in low voices, and I could hear the thin stream of tea being poured from pot to cup and the chink of cup on saucer.

Why did they talk about it on that day? What made Mother suddenly open up to Mrs H about something that almost nobody else knew? I don't know. Perhaps Mrs H was gossiping about someone else who'd had twins, or a miscarriage, or a friend whose baby had died. I don't know, and all I have is conjecture. I couldn't hear proper sentences, just the odd word here. *Fraternal twins*, said Mother.

Died at birth, said Mother. I could hear Mrs H expressing shock and sympathy, with just a tinge of greedy curiosity. *Terribly hard*, said Mother, and I could hear something in her voice that I had never heard before, a softness, a trembling.

There was silence for a moment in the kitchen. Then Mother said something else, whispering so I could barely hear. Then I heard Mrs H's loud repetition, the shock in her voice.

"*Strangled*?"

"Asphyxiated," said Mother, a big word that I didn't understand. "By the other cord."

"Oh my goodness, how terrible."

"*He* came out first," said Mother. "But by then it was too late."

Their voices sank again. I held my breath, straining my ears to try and hear more but the only thing that I heard clearly was the name *John*.

"His name was John," said Mother, and then I heard the shift and scrape of a chair as she pushed it back from the kitchen table, and I turned and fled.

Up in my room, I looked out of the window at the quiet street beyond, unseeing. Most of what had just passed was too big for me to grasp, but I must have retained the elements, the crux of it must have sunk deep into my psyche, because from that day forward, I often found myself thinking of John, of the brother I'd never known, the one who'd been with me when I was born.

For years I knew a part of me was missing. But there was something else too, something that grew and grew with me, a blackly blooming knowledge that lodged deep inside me and spread its dirty tentacles through my mind. I was born a killer, it seemed. There was no escape from that fact.

Chapter Fourteen

KATE SLEPT WITH HER MOBILE phone by her bedside, relying on the alarm clock function every morning to get her out of bed. The ringing woke her from a deep sleep, and she grabbed at the device, peering blearily at the screen. It was Anderton calling.

That woke her up. She sat up in bed and pressed the answer button.

"Kate," said Anderton. She could hear something in his voice, something that tightened her stomach, just from that one word. Something had happened.

"What's wrong?"

Anderton said nothing for a moment, but she could hear him breathing heavily. She found she was clutching the duvet cover in her free hand.

"What is it?"

"There's been another killing. Another girl."

Kate closed her eyes briefly. As the first wave of shock subsided, a thought struck her.

"But, Father Michael—"

"Is still in custody. Yes."

"Fuck," said Kate.

"Fuck indeed," said Anderton. "I need you down here right away. We're at Charlotte Street, the alley that runs along the back of it. Can you get here soon?"

"I'm on my way," said Kate, already scrambling out of bed.

The drive to Charlotte Street was a short one. Despite the warmth of the summer morning, Kate felt cold. She pressed herself back into the car seat, almost shivering. Another killing. *Another* one. And it had happened while they were questioning the wrong man. After a moment, she turned the heater on and adjusted the vent so that warm air blew onto her face.

She parked a few streets away from Charlotte Street. As Kate got out of the car, she could hear the choppy roar of a helicopter overhead. As she rounded the corner, the blue and white crime scene tape was almost invisible behind the seething mass of photographers, camera crews and journalists all vying for an interview – or better yet, a glimpse of the body, thankfully shrouded by a white tent. Kate set her features to neutral, took a deep breath and pushed through the tumult, ducking under the tape while a fusillade of camera flashes went off around her.

Anderton, Olbeck and Jerry were all in the tent,

all looking at the body. Kate joined them without speaking. Looking at the small, curled shape on the dirty concrete, she was overcome with a sense of sick, sweeping déjà vu. The long, dark hair, the slender body...just like Mandy. Just like Claudia. Kate crossed her arms across her body, hugging herself. Who was this man who kept killing women? What was driving him on? How could they catch him, and what would happen if they couldn't? Kate felt something unusual, something almost akin to panic. How could they stop him? How many more women were going to die?

She wheeled around and went back out of the tent. Cameras flashed and she flinched, unable to help herself. Trapped between the tent and the phalanx of photographers, Kate hesitated, not even sure of where she wanted to go. She heard the flap of the tent entrance again and then Anderton was behind her, beside her. He put a hand under her elbow and steered her out of the view of the press pack, around and out of sight to where his car was parked. Gesturing for her to get in the front passenger seat, he closed the door after her and went around to the driver side door.

Once he was in the car with the doors closed, they sat in silence for a moment. Then Anderton reached over and took Kate's hand. Kate glanced around nervously, hoping no one could see them.

Then Anderton spoke.

"I'm lost, Kate. I don't know what to do."

There was something in his voice. It was barely perceptible but enough to make Kate's feelings of anxiety rise up a notch. He sounded – could it be possible? – as if he were close to tears.

"Three women have died, and I have absolutely no idea who killed them."

"I know," said Kate, helplessly. "I know what you mean."

Anderton raised his head and looked her in the eyes.

"What the hell do we do?"

So now it's 'we?' Kate forced the rogue thought down. This wasn't the time for recriminations. She shrugged.

"We keep digging. We keep questioning."

Anderton sighed and leant his head back against the headrest of the car seat, closing his eyes.

"The press is going to have a field day," he said, after a moment. "They'll rip us apart. I can see the headlines now."

"I know."

"The Chief Constable is going to have my balls on a stick."

"I know."

Anderton opened his eyes, gazing at the car roof.

"All right," he said. "Let's get back there. There must be *something*. Something we're missing."

They braved the photographers again and ducked back into the tent. Doctor Telling had arrived and was leaning over the body of the woman. Olbeck and Jerry were stood to one side, not speaking.

Kate realised she hadn't even asked who the victim was.

"We don't know," said Anderton. "No ID on the body, no handbag. Just like the others."

Kate moved around a little so she could see the girl's face, dreading the moment of recognition. But it never came; this woman was a stranger.

"I've not seen her before," she said.

"She's not from the Mission?"

"Not that I can remember."

Anderton looked at Olbeck, who shook his head.

"I can't remember seeing her there either."

Anderton brought one hand up to his temple, as if afflicted by a sudden headache.

"He's escalating," he said. "It's days since the last murder. *Days*, not weeks."

Nobody said anything for a moment.

Incredibly, Anderton smiled, a grim smile that was more like a grimace. He looked at his officers.

"This is good. It means he's getting careless. It means he'll make mistakes."

Jerry said nothing. Kate looked at him curiously. The white canvas of the tent gave everyone within it a pallid hue but, Kate suddenly realised, Jerry was worse than that. He was grey. He was staring fixedly at the body as Doctor Telling was beginning her examination. His hand crept up to his shoulder, squeezing his upper arm.

Kate was just about to ask him if he was all right when Anderton spoke his name, sharply.

"Jerry? Jerry!"

Jerry dropped like a stone. Kate gasped. Frozen to the spot for a moment, movement returned, and she leapt forward at the same time as Olbeck and Anderton. Jerry had fallen next to the body, the arm that had gripped his shoulder falling loose, as if pointing towards the dead girl. There was a moment of pure chaos, people shouting, pushing. Anderton got to Jerry first, calling his name in a voice ragged with panic, before Doctor Telling moved him aside with practised authority and laid her fingers on Jerry's neck. Then she put one slender, long-fingered hand under his neck, tipping his face upwards, and began mouth to mouth resuscitation.

"Call an ambulance," she gasped as she came up for air, but Olbeck was already doing just that.

Kate, barely knowing what she was doing, took Anderton's arm, drawing him away from where Doctor Telling was battling death before their eyes.

"He'll be okay," she whispered, just for something to say. She didn't believe it for a moment. Anderton took her hand, crushing it within his grip. They watched, helplessly, for what felt like endless hours before they heard the siren of the ambulance over the bay of the mob outside the tent.

Anderton went in the ambulance, with Kate and Olbeck following behind in Kate's car. Several photographers followed the ambulance, breaking away from the crime scene when they realised there was another element to the story breaking right there. Kate crawled through the mass of people blocking the road as she tried to keep the ambulance in sight. Hands thumped on the side of the car, making her flinch. Olbeck rolled down the passenger side window.

"Clear the road. Now!"

Kate put her hand on the horn and kept it there. Wincing, people began to fall back so she could pick up a little speed. She had to fight the urge to put her foot down hard on the accelerator and drive through, scattering paparazzi like confetti.

When they got to the Royal Abbeyford Hospital, Jerry had already been carted off somewhere. *The Intensive Care Unit*, thought Kate, hoping he had at least made it that far. Anderton was in a side room off the main reception area, pacing the small area of tiled floor like a man possessed. Kate came through the doorway first, and he came forward as if to throw his arms around her, bringing himself to a sudden halt as Olbeck followed her through the doorway.

"You all right?" said Olbeck.

"I'm fine," Anderton muttered.

Kate hugged her arms across her body. The three of them stood in a little huddle, not knowing what to do or what to say.

"Well, we can't all stay," said Anderton. "Christ, I've got a serial murder investigation to run."

"It's all right," said Olbeck. "I'll stay. I'll ring you later with a progress report and someone can come and take over."

"Doesn't he have any family?" asked Kate.

Anderton shook his head. "No immediate family. All right, Mark. Let's do that. Come on Kate. I'll drive."

They drove back in silence except for one outburst from Anderton while they were waiting at the traffic lights. He pounded the steering wheel with a fist, making Kate jump.

"I *told* him, the stupid idiot. I told him. 'You drink too much, you smoke like a chimney, you eat shit...' What did he think was going to happen?"

Kate knew it was a rhetorical question. She said nothing but shrugged and shook her head.

"Stupid *idiot*," said Anderton, and then the lights changed and they were off.

When they got back to the office, the atmosphere was palpable. Jane's eyelids were as red as her hair, and Rav and Theo were looking very sombre. As

Anderton and Kate came into the room, everyone, bar Theo, leapt to their feet.

"He's still alive," said Anderton wearily. "That's about all we know for now. The doctors are doing all they can for him, and Mark will give us an update as soon as he hears."

"Was it a heart attack?" asked Jane, timidly.

Anderton nodded.

"We think so. Almost certainly."

He walked up to the notice boards and stood before then, regarding the mess of scribbled notes, photographs, documents, connecting arrows and other information.

"Where to start?" was what Kate heard him say to himself, almost under his breath.

"We've got a tentative ID on the latest victim," said Rav and Anderton turned, his eyebrows raising.

"You have? Excellent."

"A Mrs Pauline Brennan reported her daughter Karen missing after she failed to return home last night. We spoke to her over the phone, and we're bringing her in to ID the body right now."

"Fits the description?"

Rav nodded.

"Small, long dark hair, young. She – Karen – went out clubbing with friends last night, she was supposed to get the last train home. Her friends say she left to catch it, but she never went home."

"And that alleyway is the shortcut home from the

station. Sounds like it's her all right. Poor woman." Anderton sat down on the edge of a desk. "Let's get a positive ID before we do anything else. What else have we got? Anyone got any more information?"

Work went on that afternoon, but there was little sense of anything being accomplished. Jerry's desk stood horribly empty. At three o'clock, Kate texted Olbeck to see if there was any news, and he texted back, *still in ICU, no other news x.*

Mrs Pauline Brennan identified the body of her daughter, Karen Brennan, with the calmness of what Kate recognised as complete and total shock. The identification over, Mrs Brennan walked back out into the corridor and promptly collapsed, prompting another dramatic five minutes where officers swarmed, shouted and eventually ushered in the paramedics who, thankfully, advised after a few minutes' examination that the poor woman had merely fainted.

House to house enquiries were continuing along the alleyway where the body of Karen Brennan had been found and in all the neighbouring streets. CCTV footage from the train station and along Charlotte Street was being examined. Kate sat at her desk and briefly imagined herself as the spider in the centre of an enormous web of information: words, pictures, data, number plates, descriptions, interviews, forensic examinations, post mortem reports... all of it flowing to her and over her while she drowned within the torrent, snatching vaguely with her hands at scraps of knowledge that took her no further.

And out there, hidden by the darkness of ignorance, was a man who killed women and who kept killing women, and she couldn't see how they would ever catch him.

J's diary

THE MASK IS SLIPPING. I can no longer rely on my disguise. No, that's not true. Of course I can rely on my disguise – no one can see through that – but at the same time, the real me, the one underneath the mask is beginning to surface. I am transforming. For months I could always chose who to be; it was me who decided which face to present to the world, but that is beginning to be the case no longer.

Now, when I look in the mirror, I'm no longer sure of who I will see looking back.

This scares me. The real me, the one who does these things to these girls, is the one who will not be accepted. They – and I don't need to say exactly who 'they' are – they will stop me, if they catch me. They cannot catch me. I cannot allow it.

But who do I mean when I say 'I'?

This last one scared me. I hadn't planned it, I wasn't even truly looking. I was merely walking back from the station, and I saw her walk into the alleyway, staggering a little. She was the right type:

she was alone, she was drunk. All my objections fell away in an instant. Before I could tell myself that it was too dangerous, that someone would see, that she would call out or do something to call attention to what was happening...all of my internal objections counted for nothing. I was seized with the breathless, choking feeling that was beginning to come upon me more and more. I can no more conquer the urge than I could stop breathing. My feet, seemingly of their own accord, turned to follow the girl into the alleyway.

There was no one else there – of course not, it was very late. I had taken a late train back to the town and of course, I was in my usual disguise. I entered the alleyway. I like to think that if someone else had been there to witness what was about to happen, I could have controlled myself.

I like to think that, but I'm not sure.

There was no one else there. I had the knife in my hand, and I was running before I could even acknowledge what I was doing. I fell upon her from behind – she gave one small choked cry of surprise – and then the knife was going in, again and again and again. I was frenzied, my cries muffled against her back.

When it was over, I got up and staggered home. I didn't even look behind me. It makes me shudder now, to think of all the evidence I left behind me. That's what scares me. I lost control and I know – I *know* that it will happen again. I can't be caught. But I can't stop.

I can't stop.

Chapter Fifteen

KATE PULLED UP OUTSIDE HER house at about twenty minutes to seven that night. She locked the car, pulled her bag onto her shoulder and wearily made her way indoors. The house seemed very silent. She threw her bag on the floor of the hallway, kicked off her shoes and slumped through to the living room where she flung herself down onto the sofa, fully intending not to move from that location for the rest of the evening, possibly even the rest of the night.

The doorbell rang five minutes later, and she swore so loudly she was surprised the person on the doorstep didn't hear it. Kate lay, eyes closed and muttering curses under her breath, before heaving herself up and stomping through to the front door.

She yanked it open to find Andrew Stanton on the doorstep, smartly dressed and carrying a bouquet of pink roses. To Kate's tired eyes, the unexpected nature of the sight was such that for a moment she thought she was seeing things...until memory came crashing back.

Andrew took in her dishevelled, clearly-not-dressed-for-a-date appearance, and the smile he'd been wearing when the door opened fell off his face so fast it would have been funny had it not been so embarrassing.

"You forgot," was all he said.

"I'm sorry. *God*, I'm sorry." Kate was hanging onto the door as if it were the only thing keeping her from collapse. After the horrors of the day, this added complication was about as much as she could bear.

"That's fine," said Andrew, stiffly. "Perhaps another night, Kate. Good night."

He turned away, flowers dangling from his hand.

"Wait!" Kate caught at his arm to stop him. "Wait, *please*, Andrew. I'm sorry, okay? Why don't you come in?"

Once he was inside the hallway, Kate shut the front door and leant on it.

"I'm really, really sorry," she said again. "I can guess you've seen what's been happening?"

"I have," admitted Andrew. "I guess I should have phoned ahead. My fault."

"No, *completely* mine," said Kate. She felt like hitting herself sharply on the forehead. Was there a single working relationship that she hadn't managed to fuck up completely? "I hope you haven't booked anywhere...?"

Andrew half-smiled. "Well—"

"Oh, God. Where?"

"Well – Bailey's."

"Oh, *God*." Bailey's was an extremely expensive restaurant located in a former stately home on the edge of Abbeyford. "That's lovely of you. Tell you what, wait here and give me ten minutes. *Literally* ten minutes."

She virtually pushed him through to the living room, ran through to the kitchen, poured him a glass of what she always thought of as 'Mark's wine,' kept exclusively for him, ran back through – carefully – with glass in hand, set it on the living room table, smiled brightly, said 'ten minutes!' and pelted for the stairs.

After a minute's shower, a frantic rub down, a squoosh of perfume and a slick of eyeliner, she grabbed her velvet jeans and silk shirt from the wardrobe, pulled them on, dragged a brush through her hair, plucked her one smart jacket from the hanger, yanked her strappy sandals from under the bed and pounded back down the stairs, arriving flushed but hopefully less dishevelled in the doorway of the living room.

Andrew was still clutching his bouquet of flowers. He didn't look like he'd had much wine. He looked up as Kate appeared, and his face softened.

"Wow. That's a transformation."

"I'm really sorry about forgetting," said Kate, making a mental note that she was no longer going to apologise.

It looked as though Andrew had forgiven her already. He stood up and handed her the flowers.

"That's lovely," said Kate. She couldn't imagine Anderton giving her flowers. The contrast made her clench her teeth for a millisecond before she put all thoughts of him far from her.

Andrew nodded.

"You look really lovely, Kate," he said and the warmth and sincerity of his tone made Kate smile with pleasure, despite her tiredness.

"Come on, then," she said. "Let's go."

OLBECK WALKED INTO THE OFFICE the next morning to catch Kate halfway through an enormous yawn.

"I know how you feel," he said, slinging himself into his seat opposite hers.

Kate shut her mouth with a snap. She looked at her colleague, noting the bruised half-circles beneath his eyes. Looking around the room, she thought, *We all look terrible. We're all running on empty.* It was no longer surprising that Jerry had suffered a heart attack; what was surprising was that the rest of the team was all somehow managing to keep going despite the unrelenting pressure and stress.

"I'm knackered," she said, rubbing her eyes. "How's Jerry?"

"No change. They kept telling me he was stable, but they wouldn't say much else." He gestured to a small plastic bag he'd put on his desk. "I've got his stuff here. Apparently someone needs to go and get him some night clothes or something like that."

Kate yawned again, barely listening. She was wondering whether to mention her date with Andrew Stanton. Normally of course, that would set her up for at least half an hour of teasing from Olbeck, but looking at him this morning, she didn't think he'd have the energy for even a mild joke.

Not that there was much to tell. The dinner had been pleasant enough, the food very good, and Andrew had been charming and attentive company. He'd dropped her off at home at about ten o'clock and given Kate a gentlemanly kiss on the cheek on the doorstep. At least Kate thought he had; her memories by then were somewhat hazy because she'd been almost hallucinating from tiredness.

She decided against mentioning it.

Olbeck was saying something to her.

"What?"

"I said, someone needs to go and get Jerry's things for him. Pyjamas and toothbrush and all that gubbins."

"Toothbrush? He's in intensive *care*, for God's sake, he's hardly going to care about tooth decay." Kate saw Olbeck's face and relented. "Okay, okay. I'll go if you like. I could do with getting out of here."

"Thanks. It won't take long. Just drop them off at the reception area, I think."

"Fine," said Kate, yawning yet again. She took Jerry's house keys from Olbeck, scribbled down his home address and picked up her bag.

Driving through the sunshine, negotiating the weekend traffic in Abbeyford, Kate found it hard to believe that somewhere out there in the town was a multiple murderer. Everyone on the streets looked so ordinary, so innocent, so untouched. Kate braked for a pedestrian crossing – a mother with a baby in a pushchair raised a hand in thanks and pushed the buggy across the road. For once, Kate didn't look at the baby; she looked at the woman pushing the pram, who was small and thin with long, dark hair. Was she a potential victim?

For a mad moment, Kate considered parking the car and following the woman home, just to make sure she was safe. Then she shook her head, bringing herself back to reality. *You have to catch this man*, she told herself. Because he's a killer...and because if you don't, you're going to end up in a mental hospital. We all will.

Despite the sat nav, she still got lost looking for Jerry's house, which was in a suburb of Abbeyford called Fenwick. The street was quite similar to the one on which Kate lived: rows of semi-detached Victorian houses with tiny front gardens, some of which had been paved or gravelled over to provide parking spaces. Kate had to shunt her car into a tiny space on the end of the row of back-to-back vehicles and then walk back to Number Twelve, which apparently was where Jerry lived.

Kate paused at the entrance to the front garden. The house had an uncared-for look: peeling paint on the window frames, a weed-choked patch of earth in front of the front bay window. There were yellowing net curtains hanging limply at the window of the downstairs rooms. Kate checked the scrap of paper on which she'd written the address, suddenly convinced she'd got the wrong house.

No, this was definitely Jerry's place. She found the house keys and walked up the little path to the porch and the front door, tripping over a loose paving slab, catching herself and looking around self-consciously in case anyone had been watching her. There was no one in sight. Kate tried the keys in the door and pushed it open, cautiously.

The house had the kind of dusty, stale, cooking-remnants aroma that Kate, rightly or wrongly, associated with elderly people's homes. The hallway was tiled in chipped red clay tiles, probably original, with the walls papered in a faded floral pattern. Kate stood for a moment, looking around, puzzled. Again, the feeling that she'd come to the wrong house resurfaced. This, surely, was not the home of a middle-aged man. She looked around again.

There, hanging on a coat rack of dark, polished wood, was a coat she recognised as one of Jerry's. Several pairs of black and brown men's brogues were tumbled carelessly in a corner by the door. Mentally shrugging, Kate walked through the doorway at the end of the hallway that led into a kitchen.

The kitchen was quite large but had clearly been refitted about thirty years ago, judging by the orange hue of the pine cabinets and the cheap, overly-shiny brass handles. The sink and counter were piled with dirty dishes. The floor was covered in drips of unidentifiable liquid, fluff, dust and scraps of tissue paper, while in the corner by the back door, empty beer cans and bottles were stacked in a collapsing cardboard box.

Another wooden door with an old-fashioned metal latch stood under the slope of the staircase, clearly leading to what had been the cellar. Kate observed the squalor, feeling something very much like pity rising up inside her. This was Jerry's house, his empty, lonely, dirty house. What a place to come back to after doing the job they did; it was cheerless, comfortless, without any company to render it more palatable.

Kate thought of what Anderton had said about Jerry. *He's had a hard year... No immediate family.* Poor Jerry. Now, his rudeness, grumpiness, abruptness – whatever you could call it – was more understandable. Kate thought of her own house, full of carefully chosen, beautiful things (nothing very expensive, but that wasn't the point); she'd made a home for herself with love and care and attention. Was this slightly queasy feeling of pity something more? Did Jerry and she have something in common? *You're both alone*, whispered a mean little voice.

She left the kitchen and looked quickly into the other rooms on the ground floor. She wasn't sure why she was bothering. *Just being nosy, Kate.* The living room was dim and musty, worn brown velvet curtains drawn against the sunlight, the net curtains between them and the window pane no cleaner when seen from this side of the window.

There was a silver-framed photograph on the mantelpiece of what was clearly a much younger Jerry, a quite startlingly handsome Jerry. Kate stared. She wouldn't have recognised the overweight, balding, angry middle-aged man in this picture of a dark-haired, dark-eyed young charmer, smiling at the camera. She picked it up to look more closely and then looked up at herself, framed in the dusty mirror over the mantelpiece. For a second, she seemed to see herself in twenty years' time: her skin wrinkled and blotched, her dark, shiny hair dulled and greyed. She put the photograph back, repressing a shudder.

She headed for the stairs, thinking that she'd already wasted too much time here. Why on Earth had she offered to come and do this? Jerry would hate to think of her poking around in his cupboards and drawers, finding his toiletries. Kate was uncomfortably aware that she'd offered to do this precisely so she could legitimately get out of having to visit the hospital to do her shift of waiting for news like an anxious relative. She reached the top landing and pushed open the door of what was obviously the master bedroom. *"Master"* bedroom, what a stupid, sexist term. Kate shook her head.

Again, the curtains were drawn against the sunlight, and the room had that stale, musty smell of a place uncleaned, unaired, and neglected. The smell of dust and something else, something ranker underneath it all. Kate wrinkled her nose. She hesitated for a second and crossed over to the window, pulling the curtains back enough to let a little light into the room. The bed was unmade, the duvet in its sombre navy blue cover tumbled in a heap at the foot of the mattress.

Kate opened the bedside cabinet, as it was the only piece of furniture with drawers in the room.

Working on the fairly reasonable assumption that Jerry might keep his nightwear next to the bed, she regarded the contents of the drawers with raised eyebrows. Each one was rammed to the top with porn: DVDs, videos, even the odd magazine. Kate grimaced and pushed them back with her foot. She straightened up and looked around the room. No chest of drawers, no tallboy. There was a cheap, flat-pack wardrobe over by the far wall. Kate opened one door, swept her gaze over the clothes hanging up and then opened the other door.

For a moment, she looked at what was contained within with no emotion. Later, when she was to replay this moment in her head, Kate realised it had reminded her of a case she'd been working on in Bournemouth, the murder of a homeless drug addict. The victim had been found in a derelict house, and when Kate had arrived on the scene and viewed the body, she had for a few seconds wondered why there were a pair of white gloves on the victim's chest. It had taken about twenty seconds of innocent perusal before she realised that the gloves were in fact his hands, cut off at the wrist and dropped contemptuously onto his body.

Looking at the interior of Jerry's wardrobe produced a similar response. A few moments of vague puzzlement before the thumping weight of reality crashed down.

There were two handbags in the wardrobe: one

white, one black. Both, except for their colour, were identical. Fringed and tasselled, pockmarked with cheap metal studs. Kate could recall very clearly where she had last seen the black bag: over the slender shoulder of Claudia Smith.

Chapter Sixteen

KATE BREATHED IN SLOWLY. SHE felt hollow, as if a heavy weight was falling through the middle of her body, leaving empty space behind it. She closed her eyes for a moment, opened them, and looked again, as if what was in front of her could be transformed into something else by the passage of a few seconds. The bags were still there. Kate heard herself make a sound, a muffled groan or a gasp. She found herself backing away, slowly, moving backwards without looking until the backs of her legs hit the edge of the bed and she collapsed onto it into a sitting position. The old springs of the mattress creaked and groaned, echoing the sound of disbelief she'd made.

It can't be true. Not Jerry. Kate found she had her eyes squeezed tightly shut again. She must be mistaken, she *must* be. She lifted her head a little, looking again at the bags within the gloom of the wardrobe. Getting up, she groped in her pocket for a clean tissue. Wrapping it around her trembling fingers, she lifted the black handbag out from the wardrobe and put it on the bed, opening the top. She could feel from the weight of it in her hand that it wasn't empty, but it was still a shock to look inside and see a fluffy pink purse, a bunch of keys, a scratched lipstick, a balled-up tissue.

The keys had a plastic key ring attached, the kind that had an opening for a small photograph. Kate turned the blank side of it over with her tissue-clad fingers. The big dark eyes of Madison Smith looked up at her from the depths of her mother's handbag. Kate heard herself again, a noise that was something between a gasp and a retch. She picked up the purse and opened it. A credit card in the name of Ms. C Smith. A debit card in the name of Claudia Smith. *No. No.*

Kate left Claudia's bag on the bed and went to fetch the white one. What had Claudia said about Mandy's bag? "*We got 'em together except Mandy's was white.*" Kate ferried it across to the bed and put it by its negative twin. Inside was a red leather purse, pens, a notebook with a geometric flower print on the cover, tissues, baby wipes, cigarettes, a packet of condoms. Kate opened the purse. Amanda Renkin was printed on the one bank card contained within it.

There must be another explanation. There *must* be. Kate sat back down on the bed, the springs groaning beneath her, and pinched the bridge of her nose. *Think, Kate. Think.* Jerry had the handbags from two murdered girls in his wardrobe. Could he have taken them from the bodies? Of course he had, how ridiculous. Of course he had taken them – how else would they have got here? Kate realised her mistake. She meant, could he have taken them from the bodies without him necessarily being the killer? And if he had, *why* had he? Why tamper with the evidence?

Kate raised her head and stared at the open door of the wardrobe. A coldness was creeping through her body, as if an icy wave were moving slowly through her. If Jerry wasn't the killer and had tampered with evidence...well, the only explanation Kate could come up with was that Jerry had done it to shield someone else. Who?

You know who, whispered that small mean voice again.

Kate shook her head. This was ridiculous. Truly ridiculous. She stood up, wobbling a little, and walked to the window, staring out at the quiet suburban street outside. A woman walked past the house with bulging supermarket shopping bags in each hand, a little boy on a scooter following behind her. Could Jerry really be the killer? Kate thought back to the last crime scene, Jerry staring at the body, grey in the face, as within him his heart ruptured. What had Anderton said? *He's escalating. He will have made mistakes.*

Had Jerry seen something then and realised that he would be caught? Had he remembered something, some piece of evidence that would point the police to his guilt? *Was* he guilty? *He must be, Kate. How else can you explain finding these handbags?*

He might be shielding someone else.

Kate realised she was pacing the dusty carpet, arguing with herself. Who would Jerry shield? Who would he risk his career, his reputation, his freedom for? She turned on her heel and paced back. There was no one. Surely, no one. *It must be him*, Kate told herself, staring at her white face in the mirrored door of the wardrobe.

Oh fuck, what was she going to do? She probably shouldn't have even touched those bags, tissue or no tissue. She looked again into the wardrobe but there was nothing else there. No other bags or purses or anything suspicious.

She pulled out her phone and brought Anderton's number up on the screen. Her thumb hovered over the 'call' button for a moment and then she pressed it, listening to the ringing on the other end of the line.

He might be shielding someone else.

Kate jabbed the 'end call' button. Her chest felt tight. She told herself she was being ridiculous. Paranoid and ridiculous. She tried to think back over the times and dates, tried to tally them up with her own memories. *Anderton was with me the night*

Claudia Smith was killed. He was with me for the whole night.

But had he been? Kate had slept for several hours. Was it conceivable that Anderton could have left her sleeping, crept out and... Surely not. It was impossible.

Other memories were creeping back. What had Anderton said when he walked her home? *There's a man who kills women on the loose in this town.* And Kate had queried the use of the plural. Why had he said 'women,' not woman? Only one woman had been killed then. She'd even said as much to him.

Kate groaned. What she was thinking was impossible. Surely it was impossible. There was no way that Anderton could have left her room, driven to the factory wastelands, somehow lured Claudia there and killed her, returning in time to be there, naked in bed, when Kate woke up. Surely not?

Kate was pacing again. She stopped dead, suddenly struck by a thought that was so devastating that she thought she might faint. She sat down hurriedly on the edge of the bed again.

What if it was both of them? Anderton *and* Jerry? Of course they would have rock solid alibis for some of the murders if the other one was committing them.

What you're thinking is madness.

Kate picked up her phone again and brought up Olbeck's number. On the verge of ringing it, she hesitated. Now that her imagination had begun working overtime, she saw News of the World headlines, tabloid fever. Was it possible that her phone was tapped? Had someone been leaking information to the media? She thought of the scrum of photographers that they'd driven through yesterday.

In the end, she sent him a text that read: *need to see you here at Jerry's URGENTLY. Can't talk over phone. COME HERE ASAP!*

After she put the phone back in her pocket, Kate stood for a moment in the middle of Jerry's fetid bedroom, hugging her arms across her body. Despite the dusty, prickling heat of the room, she felt cold. She could feel her lungs fluttering within her, her breath coming in short, tight bursts.

Realising she was three steps away from a panic attack, she forced herself to sit down again on the edge of the bed, drop her head forward and breathe deeply, in through her nose and out through her mouth. She kept this up until her hammering heart had slowed a little and she felt very slightly calmer. The buzzing in her ears receded.

The house seemed very quiet. Kate sat for a moment longer, trying to keep hold of the momentary calmness. Now that the thoughts in her head had settled a little, she became more aware of her surroundings, the dust flying in the shafts of sunlight that lanced through the gap in the dirty curtains. The smell of the room filled her nostrils. A thought struck her which made her heartbeat speed up again to alarming levels.

What if there were more bodies in the house?

Kate leapt up, her hand to her mouth. Her imagination was flying again, bringing up all sorts of hideous pictures. She thought again of tabloid headlines, pictures of erstwhile normal suburban houses that had concealed a raft of horrors. Would the paparazzi be camped outside this innocuous-looking Victorian terrace tomorrow morning? Of course they would. Perhaps they were already on their way. But how could they be?

Kate no longer knew what she actually knew or what she had conjectured. She felt dizzy with the enormity of what had happened. Where the hell was Olbeck? She breathed in sharply, and the room smelt even ranker than it had before. Kate backed away from the bed, eyeing the dark space beneath it. She stood for a moment, indecisively, wringing her sweaty hands. She knew she should look under the bed. She knew she should, but she quailed from the idea. Although it was unusual, she was afraid to look. *Come on, Kate. What could be as bad as what you're imagining?*

She took a deep breath, almost gagged and dropped to her knees with a thump, peering into the murk, sweating with fear. There was nothing under the bed but clumps of dust and hairs, an empty shoe box and a plastic biro. Nothing there. Kate sat back up, her in-held breath rushing out in one long sigh.

She checked her phone. Nothing from Olbeck. Nothing from Anderton. Her fevered speculation about her boss was beginning to die away. Surely it was too ludicrous a thought even to be entertained?

All of a sudden, Kate knew she had to get out of the house. Another minute here in this fetid, dusty atmosphere would see her lose the plot. She hurried downstairs, prickling with fear, terrified of what she might see in the corner of her eye. She closed and locked the front door behind her and stood for a moment on the porch, taking in great gulps of fresh air.

Her relief at being outside the house was so great that it took her a moment or two to realise that someone was talking to her, addressing her by name.

"—Redman?"

Kate blinked. The woman speaking to her from the pavement was vaguely familiar, but Kate's current emotional state was such that she couldn't place her. After a moment, thankfully, her memory returned.

"Hello, Miss Paling."

Margaret Paling was looking at her curiously.

"What brings you hear, dear?"

"Do you live near here?" asked Kate, countering with a question. Margaret waved a hand at the row of houses opposite.

"My house is over there. Number Fifteen. This is Jerry's Hindley's house, isn't it? Didn't he mention we were neighbours?"

Had he? Kate felt so battered by the revelations of the past hour that she couldn't remember.

Margaret was still looking at her with concern.

"Are you all right, dear? You're as white as a sheet. Quite as white as a sheet."

Kate opened her mouth to say 'I'm fine,' but somehow the words wouldn't come out properly.

"Why don't you come over and have a cup of tea?" asked Margaret. "Or a glass of water, or something. Seriously, dear, you look like you're about to faint."

Kate opened her mouth again to refuse politely and then thought better of it. If this woman was Jerry's neighbour, it was possible she might have witnessed something. *At the very least*, Kate thought, *I'll be able to find out a little bit more about Jerry's background.*

"Yes, I will. Thank you."

Chapter Seventeen

Number Fifteen, Smithson Street, was almost a carbon-copy of Jerry's house in age, layout, décor and furnishing, except it was considerably cleaner and had none of the masculine accoutrements lying about. Margaret ushered Kate through the main hallway into a neat and tidy kitchen and sat her down at the table. She kept up a stream of inconsequential chatter as she prepared the tea, the words washing over Kate in a rather soothing stream that she barely heard. The kettle boiled and the water was poured into a fine china teapot to brew. Margaret handed Kate a plate of biscuits.

"I think you should have one of those, dear. Sugar's very good if you're feeling a bit shaky."

She hadn't yet asked what had so upset Kate. Kate wasn't sure what she was going to say if Margaret did ask the question.

The tea was hot and strong, and Kate drank it gratefully.

"Do you know Jerry well?" she asked.

"Not very well, I must say. We're neighbourly. Friendly but not *friends*, if you see what I mean." Margaret took a sip from her own cup. "How is he? We've all been rather worried about him."

"Oh, you know he's in hospital?"

"Yes, Mrs Culson at Number Nine told me yesterday. Poor man, he's not had a good year, what with his bereavement and everything else."

"Bereavement?"

"Yes, dear. His mother died, oh, it must be six months ago now. Terribly hard, isn't it, when you lose a family member? I lost my own mother last year, and it does take a while to get over it."

"I'm sorry," said Kate automatically. She was going to say "I didn't know" and then realised how callous and ridiculous that sounded. How could she not have known Jerry lost his mother? Why hadn't anyone told her?

The knowledge of what Jerry had done thumped her in the stomach again, and she put the remainder of her biscuit down on the little plate in front of her.

Margaret Paling chatted on.

"Of course, it's hard being on your own. I had Jerry over for dinner a few times, and I think it helped. He's always struck me as a bit of a lonely person. Very much keeps to himself."

The stuff of cliché: the quiet killer, the respectable murderer. Kate felt a hysterical giggle rise up inside her, and she coughed, a hand to her mouth. For a horrible second, she thought she wouldn't be able to control herself – she could feel raucous laughter rising up her throat – and she swallowed, crookedly, which hurt and helped to push the feeling down.

She wasn't sure Margaret had noticed. The other woman was engaged in pouring out the last drops of tea into Kate's cup.

Kate swallowed, and then swallowed again and cleared her throat.

"Have you lived here long?" she asked, once she could be sure of her voice.

Margaret set the empty pot back on the table.

"Around here? My whole life, dear. My mother and father bought this house before the war, I believe. I was actually born here."

"That's nice," said Kate, automatically. She wanted to check her phone to see if Olbeck or Anderton had tried to contact her, but she couldn't think of a way to do it without looking rude.

"Yes, I've seen a lot of changes in the town over the years. Not always for the better either. But never mind me. I'm just an old woman stuck in my ways."

Kate smiled again and did a sort of half shake of the head. What was there to say to a remark like that? An agreement was rude and a negation didn't sound right either.

"You're looking a wee bit better," said Margaret.

"Now, would you like some more tea? Or I can make coffee, if you prefer?"

Kate managed a smile.

"You're very kind," she said, "But please don't worry. That cup did me good, and that's all I needed, thank you."

"That's no problem. Happy to help."

Margaret stood up.

"Now, would you excuse me for a moment, dear? I have to go to the little girl's room."

For some reason she giggled, a rather odd, girlish sound. Kate nodded and smiled automatically, her mind on something else.

When Margaret had left the room, Kate sat, trying to pin down what it was that was making her uneasy. Something that Margaret had said, just now. What was it? Something... something about *coffee*. That was it. What was it about coffee that was important?

Kate stared ahead, her fingers unconsciously tapping the table. Coffee and Rav – something Rav had said. What the hell was it? After a moment of blankness, the memory returned. Rav and she had been sitting in the car, and she'd wanted to stop for a coffee. That was it. Rav had joked about her throwing a drink in his face, because she'd done that to Jerry the night before. What an idiot she'd been.

Kate frowned, unsure of why her brain was telling

her this was so important. Then comprehension dawned. After he'd joked about the coffee, Rav had said something about going clubbing: *that he and Jerry and the others had been at a club all night.* Hadn't he said something about it being daylight by the time they left? That was the night Claudia Smith was killed. How could Jerry have killed her when he was with the other officers at a nightclub for the entire night?

For a moment, Kate felt as if her brain had actually given way under the strain. If Jerry hadn't killed Claudia, then who had? Who had killed the other women? Who?

Kate came back to reality with a start, unsure of how long she'd been sitting at the table, staring into space and drumming her fingers on the edge. She looked around. The house seemed very silent. Where had Margaret gone?

Kate got up and stretched. It was time for her to go, but she should say goodbye first. She went out into the hallway and looked around, listening for sounds of movement. There was nothing. Kate hesitated. There was a tiny thread of uneasiness running through her, some almost subconscious sense of something not being quite right. Was it something else that Margaret had said?

Kate began to climb the stairs, thinking hard. Something about Margaret that rang another faint bell. What was it? For a moment, Kate feared she had actually gone mad, the fear and strain of the past few hours taking their toll. Was she being paranoid? She climbed further, treading softly, the old polished wood of the banister sliding smoothly under her palm.

Kate reached the top of the stairs. Through a half-open door to the right, she could see the edge of a bath, a sink, a tiled floor. That was the bathroom, but it looked empty. Where was Margaret? Had she actually come upstairs?

Kate shifted from foot to foot, standing at the top of the stairs. The old floorboards creaked under her feet. That sense of uneasiness was growing – in fact, it was almost fear. What was there to be afraid of? Was it the silent house, the disappearance of her hostess – or something else?

Beyond the bathroom door was another door. Kate tiptoed towards it and pushed it gently open. It opened into what was obviously the master bedroom. Kate hesitated in the doorway, unsure of what she was doing or what she would find. The room was empty, the double bed made neatly with a pink candlewick bedspread tucked across it. At the far wall was a small, wooden dressing table with an adjustable mirror on the top. On the surface of the dressing table, on a white lace doily, was a small, wooden jewellery box.

As soon as Kate saw it, she knew what she'd been thinking of. *Brooches*. Margaret's rhinestone brooch. Without stopping to think, Kate strode forward until she reached the dressing table and lifted the lid of the jewellery box.

A part of her had been expecting what she saw, but still she heard herself gasp. Again, she had that feeling of freefall, something heavy moving downwards through her body, leaving her weak and trembling. The dark interior of the jewellery box could not quite dim the blue shine of the butterfly brooch within it. Kate stared at it, seeing again the bruise on Ingrid Davislova's skin. She could hear the roar of her heartbeat in her ears, pounding like a bass drum, but even beyond that, she was suddenly aware of something, some other sound just on the edge of hearing: a whisper of a footstep in the corridor outside, the faint hiss of an indrawn breath.

Time stood still for a moment. Kate's horrified gaze rose slowly, from the jewellery box to the mirror. There was a flicker in the glass and a dark shape rushed at her from behind, growing larger with terrifying speed.

Already pumped full of adrenaline, Kate's body reacted before her mind did. She darted sideways just as the figure crashed into the dressing table, making the mirror rock back against the wall. As she turned to run, Kate caught sight of her attacker, dressed in an old-fashioned men's suit and hat that shadowed the face.

Despite her shock, Kate was thinking it must be an unknown relative of Margaret's: a son, a brother. Seconds later, the hat fell off as the person rushed forward, and Kate saw the face; it was Margaret's face but it had been distorted, teeth bared, eyes glaring. She was so shocked that she almost didn't register the knife before it came down in a sweeping rush that Kate, feinting right, barely escaped.

Sobbing with fear, Kate turned, scrambling for the door before slamming it shut in Margaret's maniacal face. Kate ran for her life, slipping a little at the turn of corridor, stumbling down the stairs. Everything had happened so quickly that she was barely aware of anything else besides the overwhelming desire to run. She fell the last three steps, turning her ankle but hardly registering the flash of pain. Above her, she could hear the bedroom door thud back against the wall and Margaret's hissing breath as she ran after Kate. In three bounds, Kate reached the front door, scrabbled for the lock and handle, pulled.

The door was locked.

Kate had time to think about running for the back door, a second's vision of making her escape that way. Then the blow came, a hard punch to the base of her ribs, which drove the breath from her body for an instant. Margaret's body pressed up against hers from behind, pinning her to the door. There was an excruciating moment of pain as the knife went in, a shockingly intimate penetration, and then a dragging heaviness and a blooming dull heat.

Kate thought confusedly, *I'm okay, I'm okay, I've got my stab vest on*, but of course she wasn't on patrol anymore, was she? She wasn't wearing a vest. Margaret was panting loudly in her ear. Kate felt the knife pull back, leaving her body, and she thought, *She's going to stab me again*. Without thinking, she gasped for air and pushed herself backwards, bringing her head back sharply.

The back of her skull connected violently with Margaret's nose. There was a crunch and a muffled scream and then the pressure on Kate was relieved.

Margaret fell backwards, her nose gouting scarlet. Kate turned, feeling a great wash of blood from the wound in her back go flooding through her shirt, warm and wet. She staggered past Margaret, who was scrabbling to get up from the hallway floor, and limped into the first room off the hallway, the living room, before her legs gave way and she thumped down onto the carpet in front of the fire.

I'm going to die here, I'm going to die was the only thought going through her mind. Kate managed to turn over and face the doorway just in time to see Margaret, face streaked with blood, up on her feet and waving the knife. She saw Kate helpless and spread-eagled on the carpet and screamed triumphantly, running forward with the knife, ready to swoop down in the final, fatal blow.

It was Kate's legs that saved her. Strengthened and toned from weeks of training, they kicked not out, but up, catching Margaret on the run and pushing her towards the ceiling so that the momentum of her movement carried her up through the air, above Kate, to crash into the marble mantelpiece. The movement was too quick for her to cry out. Her head hit the mantelpiece, and she dropped like a stone, almost on top of Kate, who managed to roll away a little, screaming herself at the pain in her abdomen as the knife wound opened and the blood flowed.

Gasping, Kate propelled herself backwards on her elbows, pure adrenaline moving her muscles. Margaret lay, crumpled and silent, by the hearth. Kate reached the sofa, tried to pull herself up to a standing position. Was Margaret dead? Where was the knife?

Kate felt for her mobile phone in her back pocket. Every movement exploded with pain and brought with it a fresh flow of blood from the wound. She could feel her vision fogging; greyness began to creep into her line of sight. She managed to grasp the phone, brought it out, dropped it as it slithered through her bloody fingers. Breathing was becoming difficult now. Kate groaned, feeling the blood flowing like a river down her back, down her legs. Her shirt was sodden.

She took every last bit of energy, stood up and staggered to the mantlepiece. Her shaking fingers reached out to grasp the heaviest thing she could reach, a gold-framed black and white photograph. Kate gasped like a fish, took in what little breath she could and hurled the picture as hard as her fading strength would allow at the living room window.

Dimly she heard the crash of falling glass, but before the musical tinkle of the shards landing on the ground outside had faded, Kate felt herself slide forward, sinking to the blood-wet carpet as everything went black.

J's Diary

THE BUTTERFLY BROOCH IS BY my hand while I write. My eye keeps being drawn to it; this small piece of cheap, enamelled metal. I keep seeing portents in everything; the most random things become meaningful. Is this madness? There are those who would say that what I do is madness, but I don't *feel* mad. Quite the opposite. The more I kill, the more I feel in control. The cooler and calmer I get.

Perhaps that's what it's all about after all. Control.

Mother was always the one in control. There was only one time I saw her fearful. That was the day of my first transformation. The butterfly brooch had a part to play there as well; perhaps that's what reminded me.

It was last summer. For some reason, I had gone into Mother's bedroom, and the butterfly brooch was lying in the middle of her dressing table, quite alone. I stood there for several minutes, staring at it. I couldn't have said why.

There was a flicker in the glass of the dressing table mirror, and I looked up and into it to see the reflection of Mother standing in the doorway to her room, staring at me.

There was a moment's silence, oddly loaded. Our gazes met in the mirror. After a few seconds, she dropped her eyes to look at what I'd been staring at.

"Your father bought me that," she said, indicating the brooch with a nod of her white head. "On the day I found out I was pregnant with you and your brother."

I didn't say anything for a moment. John. It was the first time she'd ever acknowledged his existence to me. I was flummoxed, not only by the subject matter, but also by her tone. It was the first time in weeks she'd directed a normal, almost friendly word my way.

She walked up behind me, growing larger in the reflection. Seen side by side, our faces looked very similar despite the difference in our age. I had the strangest impression that she knew that I knew about John, about how he'd died. That she knew that I'd found the story out long before but she'd never mentioned it because she wanted me kept in suspense, in horror at what I'd done. She wanted me to be punished.

She leaned forward, smiling nastily.

"The wrong twin died," she said, almost whispering. I could feel her eyes on my face, greedy for my reaction to her words.

My face reflected nothing. After a moment, bored, she turned away and walked out of the room.

The strangest thing happened. It was as if someone else were standing behind me, as close as Mother had been. As if they stepped forward, into me. My vision blurred. All I could see before me was the hard, bright blue of the butterfly brooch. Rage flooded through me like a welcome fire.

I turned quickly and followed Mother, who was just taking a step downwards at the top of the stairs. My hands went out, but were they my hands, or John's hands? They connected with the small of Mother's back and pushed, just a quick little shove. I can still remember the feel of her birdlike ribcage under my palms for the brief second before she fell. It was the first time I'd touched her in years. She tumbled down, giving one short, sharp cry before she hit the hallway floor in a tangle of withered limbs.

I remained for a moment on the top step. Exhilaration swept through my bloodstream like a drug; I felt drunk with power. I had killed Mother.

That wasn't quite true. She was still alive when I reached the hallway floor and bent over her. Her face was twisted awkwardly, her mouth opening and shutting like a baby bird's. One grey eye blinked at me.

I leant over, watching her pupil contract. Then I smiled slowly. I backed away towards the front door, step by slow step. She made a small sound of protest, something that wasn't quite a word. Was she trying to say my name? I hadn't heard the word *Margaret* cross her lips in months. I smiled again, smiled and waved a casual goodbye. Then I went outside and locked the front door behind me.

Walking away down the quiet street, I felt my soul grow wings. I knew then that I was able to transform, to become someone different. All it took was the courage to hold death in your hands and reach out and kill. I was trembling with the realisation that *that* was the secret I had looked for for so long.

Chapter Eighteen

THERE WERE VOICES RIGHT ON the edge of hearing, but no discernible words. Just the hum and babble of human speech, heard from some distance away. Then other sounds became recognisable: the rattle of curtain rings, the clank of something metallic, the ringing of a telephone. Kate heard them all without being able to think much about them, and after a time, the noises faded and darkness came back.

When she could hear the sounds again, they were louder and more intrusive. At the same time, she became aware of something else – a warm feeling of pressure on her right hand. She struggled for a moment to open her eyes, and after a few seconds, the blurry image of a ceiling and the top of a green curtain came into view. Kate blinked and her gaze dropped to see the welcome face of Olbeck smiling down at her. It was he who was holding her hand, she realised after another moment.

"Hi," croaked Kate.

"Hello, you." Olbeck leant forward a little, squeezing her hand. "How are you feeling?"

Kate considered.

"Crap."

Olbeck smiled.

"Geez, Kate, I knew you wanted to get out of running the half marathon, but you didn't have to go *this* far."

Kate laughed weakly and then gasped as pain shot through her. She looked down at herself, fearful of what she would see. A mass of bandages was just visible under the hospital gown she was wearing.

"What happened?"

"Don't you remember?"

Kate blinked and the face of Margaret Paling swam back into view. The gleam of the knife as it came down, the warmth of the blood as it gushed out of her. Kate swallowed.

"I remember."

"That knife missed your lung by an *inch*, Kate. Someone was obviously looking out for you. You lost a lot of blood, but you'll be okay. You just need to rest and get better."

Kate felt the sudden hot surge of tears underneath her eyelids and blinked them away.

"I'll be okay?" she managed.

"You should be. You won't be running any marathons, half or otherwise, for a while."

"Silver lining," Kate said, trying to grin through her tears.

"Jay and Courtney have been here, but they had to go. I thought I'd sit with you for a while."

"Glad – glad you did." Kate was sorry she'd missed her brother and sister. She wanted to ask whether her mother had visited her but decided against it.

"What happened – afterwards?" she asked.

"After the attack?"

"Yes."

"Well, I got your text. I was in the middle of interviewing poor Karen's Brennan's mother, so I couldn't get back to you, and I couldn't leave immediately. I stopped the interview as soon as I decently could, and Anderton and I headed on over to Jerry's place. Of course, we couldn't find you anywhere, and we were starting to get a bit worried when this bloody great shower of glass explodes just down the street."

Kate smiled faintly, remembering hurling the photograph with all the remaining strength that she had. Thank God she had.

"What about Margaret?"

Olbeck looked serious.

"She's dead, Kate."

"I remember," whispered Kate. "She hit her head on the wall, on the fireplace, didn't she?"

"Well, yes. But she also fell on the knife. Talk about hoist by your own petard."

"It was – her though? The killings? She – she did them all?"

Olbeck squeezed her hand again.

"Oh, yes. We've found – well, I won't go into that now. Anderton will come and give you the run down when you're feeling a bit stronger."

"Okay." Kate could feel a heaviness dragging down her eyelids. She forced them open, fighting against a sudden great weariness.

"You're knackered," said Olbeck. "Get some rest. Me and Jeff will be back later."

He kissed her on the forehead, and Kate smiled weakly. She could still feel the warmth of his hand as she fell into unconsciousness.

Some time passed before she became aware of reality again. Like the last time, she heard the sounds of the ward before she opened her eyes, although there was no warmth of another human hand holding hers. Instead she heard her name, quite clearly.

"Kate. Kate."

Kate opened her eyes. Anderton was sitting where Olbeck had sat before.

"Welcome back," he said, smiling.

Kate tried to smile back. In truth, seeing him sat there without touching her, without holding her hand, hurt her almost as much as the healing knife wound.

"How are you feeling?"

"I've been better," said Kate, not wanting his pity.

"You did well."

"I'm just glad we caught hi—" She caught herself. "I mean, I'm glad we caught her. God, that sounds so weird, given the context."

"You're not wrong. The press are having a field day. Britain's first female serial killer and all that."

Kate rolled her eyes.

"What about Rose West? Myra Hindley?"

Anderton nodded.

"Well, there is a precedent, I suppose. But Margaret was killing on her own. Although—" He looked thoughtful. "We found her diaries. You'll have to read them when you're stronger. There's material in there that would keep a team of psychiatrists busy for decades."

He hesitated for moment.

"We found another body in the house. Searched the whole building – took it apart at the seams, obviously, after what happened. The body of a young girl, thin, dark-haired."

"Stabbed with the same knife?"

"That's right. Clearly her first victim. We know from reading her diaries that she killed her mother too. That's what started all this off."

Kate cleared her throat.

"Why did she do it?"

Anderton shrugged.

"Again, Kate, that's one for the psychiatrists. Repressed sexuality? Self-hate? Self-loathing so extreme she created a whole new persona for herself, someone who could kill women and in killing women, act out the rage and shame she had for herself? I don't know. I think it's fitting she went for victims who resembled her mother when she was young."

"Did they also resemble Margaret when she was young?"

Anderton looked startled.

"Now you mention it, that's true. Perhaps that was an element as well."

Kate was thinking.

"Why – why put the bags in Jerry's house?"

Anderton shrugged.

"She did a lot of things to throw us off the scent. Remember the condom lubricant found on Mandy's body? Nice little trick there to make us think it was a man. Well, of course we thought that anyway. Why wouldn't we?"

Kate closed her eyes momentarily. She remembered her frantic speculation on the identity of the killer after she'd found those bags. Jerry – and then Anderton. How *could* she have thought that? *That's something I'll never tell him,* she thought.

"How is Jerry?" she asked out loud.

"Better," said Anderton. Then he hesitated. "A bit better. They think he's going to pull through but...well, I don't think he'll be back at work again. But he is getting better."

"Good," said Kate and was glad she actually meant it. She wondered whether she and Jerry had been in Intensive Care together. Perhaps lying next to one another in beds side by side. What a thought...

"Their mothers were friends," Anderton was saying. "Margaret Paling's mother and Jerry's mother. That's his mother's house of course – he inherited it when she died, he's only been living there for a few months. Margaret had a key to his house which he probably didn't know about. She must have thought he'd make a good scapegoat."

Kate nodded, feeling the pillow rustle against her ears.

"She looked so harmless," she said. "I can't believe I sat across the table from her drinking tea and I had no idea. Not then. She just looked so ordinary."

"Well, that made it so easy for her, didn't it?" said Anderton. "Who on Earth would suspect a respectable elderly woman of these terrible crimes?"

"That's why it was easy for her to get her victims to the canal ground," Kate said, considering. "They trusted her. They wouldn't have been afraid of her."

"Exactly. We can't know what she told them, but I'd imagine it was quite convincing. They wouldn't have suspected her for a moment."

"Perfect disguise," said Kate.

"Exactly."

Kate sighed, thinking of the girls who had died. Could they have been saved? Could the team have done anything different? She had no doubt that there had been mistakes made that had possibly cost lives. She'd have to live with that. *I'm sorry*, she said to Mandy and Claudia and Karen inside her head.

"Thank God we caught her," she said, aloud.

"Indeed. Although, from the pace of the killings, it was likely we'd have caught her sooner rather than later anyway. She was becoming frantic."

"Right."

Anderton smiled faintly.

"That's not to do down your achievement, Kate."

"I didn't do much."

"Nonsense."

Kate couldn't be bothered to argue. She felt weak and ill. Talking about Margaret was bringing up memories of the attack.

Anderton noted her pallor.

"We'll talk about it later, Kate. It's all in hand."

"Thanks," she said, with difficulty.

"You just need to concentrate on getting better. It's not the same without you."

"Isn't it?" asked Kate. Their eyes met and for a second, she felt leap of something within her that lifted her temporarily out of her pain. It only lasted a moment before tiredness began to engulf her again.

"Get some rest," said Anderton, and the tone of his voice was such that Kate found herself smiling as she slid back into sleep. The last thing she was aware of as unconsciousness engulfed her was the warm faint pressure of his fingers as he took her hand.

THE END

Enjoyed this book? An honest review left at Amazon, Goodreads, Shelfari and LibraryThing is always welcome and *really* important for indie authors. The more reviews an independently published book has, the easier it is to market it and find new readers.

Sign up to Celina Grace's newsletter here at her website http://www.celinagrace.com for news of new releases, promotions and other goodies. You can unsubscribe at any time and won't be bombarded with emails, promise!

Twitter:
@celina__grace

Facebook:
http://www.facebook.com/authorcelinagrace

Want more Kate Redman? The new Kate Redman Mystery, **Snarl**, is now available on Amazon.

Snarl (A Kate Redman Mystery: Book 4)

A RESEARCH LABORATORY OPENS ON the outskirts of Abbeyford, bringing with it new people, jobs, prosperity and publicity to the area – as well as a mob of protestors and animal rights activists. The team at Abbeyford police station take this new level of civil disorder in their stride – until a fatal car bombing of one of the laboratory's head scientists means more drastic measures must be taken...

Detective Sergeant Kate Redman is struggling to come to terms with being back at work after long period of absence on sick leave; not to mention the fact that her erstwhile partner Olbeck has now been promoted above her. The stakes get even higher as a multiple murder scene is uncovered and a violent activist is implicated in the crime. Kate and the team must put their lives on the line to expose the murderer and untangle the snarl of accusations, suspicions and motives.

Snarl is the new Kate Redman Mystery from crime writer Celina Grace, author of Hushabye, Requiem and Imago. Available now.

Acknowledgements

MANY THANKS TO ALL THE following splendid souls:

Chris Howard for the brilliant cover designs; Brenda Errichiello for editing and proofreading; Kathy McConnell for extra proofreading; lifelong Schlockers and friends David Hall, Ben Robinson and Alberto Lopez; Ross McConnell for advice on police procedural and for also being a great brother; Kathleen and Pat McConnell, Anthony Alcock, Naomi White, Mo Argyle, Lee Benjamin, Bonnie Wede, Sherry and Amali Stoute, Cheryl Lucas, Georgia Lucas-Going, Steven Lucas, Loletha Stoute and Harry Lucas, Helen Parfect, Helen Watson, Emily Way, Sandy Hall, Kristýna Vosecká; and of course my patient and ever-loving Chris, Mabel, Jethro and Isaiah.

Printed in Dunstable, United Kingdom